A Yorkshire Christmas

A Yorkshire Christmas

A CHRISTMAS AROUND THE WORLD NOVELLA

KATE HEWITT

TULE
PUBLISHING

CHAPTER ONE

*H*OW TO HAVE A *Perfect Christmas*. Claire Lindell's mouth twisted cynically as she read the headline of the article in the airline magazine. According to the featured website *BrambleCottage.com*, there were no less than twenty-five tips to having a magical holiday. She skimmed the article, her mouth turning down as she read about how scented candles created a mood, and she should buy wrapping paper during the sales after the holidays and save it for the next year. How to make sauce from fresh cranberries, and how mashed potatoes with skimmed milk and olive oil spread were delicious *and* low calorie. A well-decorated table, using fresh evergreen and holly, could, apparently, make *all* the difference.

Claire didn't read past the first ten tips to a perfect Christmas. She'd read enough, and in any case, she'd been part of enough so-called perfect Christmases to last a lifetime.

She crammed the magazine back into the pouch in front of her and stared out the window at the endless black night. The plane was soaring at an altitude of thirty-four thousand feet, had been in the air for three and a half hours, and most of the other passengers on their way to Manchester, England from New York were asleep or trying to be.

All except Claire.

Insomnia had been her unwelcome friend for four and a half weeks, since Thanksgiving, to be precise. Since she'd gone way too far down a road she'd never thought she would have travelled.

But at least you turned back.

Sighing, she shifted restlessly in her seat. Her eyes felt gritty and hot, and her muscles ached with fatigue. She glanced down at her carry-on canvas bag, filled with final exams she needed to mark before she returned to her position as history teacher at Stirling Academy for Girls on Manhattan's rarefied Upper East Side. She couldn't face the exams yet and so she looked away, stabbing the button to power up the little screen installed in the back of the seat in front of her. Endless entertainment was what she needed. It might, at least, provide a distraction from the circling of her thoughts.

She scrolled through the offerings of films: gritty thriller, weepy drama, lighthearted rom com. No, no, no. She finally settled on a documentary about Bengali tigers and after ten minutes she closed her eyes, content to let the words just drift over her.

In just under three hours she would land in Manchester, hire a rental car to drive the hour and a half to Ledstow, a small village, thirty miles outside of York where her god-mother had a cottage. Her godmother Ruth Carrington was spending Christmas in London, and when Claire had seen Ruth's status update on Facebook, she had, in a moment of desperation borne of urgency, asked her if she could stay in Ledstow while she was away.

Ruth had said yes, as Claire had known she would. She only saw her godmother every few years, but Ruth was always effusive in her welcome and warmth, and Claire had had a standing invitation to visit England since she was eight years old.

She couldn't bear another one of her mother's perfect Christmases. The perfect tree, decorated with color-coordinated ornaments, with a different theme every year. The perfect Christmas dinner, brought in discreetly by high-end caterers. The perfect everything, and all of it completely fake, the trappings of happy family life draped over an empty husk.

Melanie Lindell had been icily disappointed that Claire, for the first time in her twenty-nine years, would not be joining the family festivities at their six-thousand-square-foot home in Greenwich, Connecticut. Claire's sister Abby would be going, of course, with her perfect husband Andrew and her two perfect children, four-year-old Andrew Junior, nicknamed Drew Drew, and six-year-old Skylar. Claire could picture them now; Drew Drew in his Rachel Riley polo shirt and crisp khakis, Skylar in Lily Pulitzer. The beautiful, perfect family, poster children for prosperity and happiness.

Claire didn't want to be around all the glossy perfection, not when she fell so short of the mark. So, she'd hole up in Ledstow, in Yorkshire, reading books and marking essays, enjoying the luxuries of solitude and quiet, a bottle of wine, and a roaring fire.

It sounded like bliss. It also sounded like hell. Claire had been alone with her thoughts for too long already, and that had been while working a full-time teaching job, preparing kids for finals and college applications, helping with the Winter Concert, doing the obligatory round of social events even though she'd felt as if she were sleepwalking through life. And that was on a good day.

Okay, enough with the self-pity. This is your downtime, and when you get back to New York, you'll have put all this heartache behind you. You'll be upbeat and purposeful and you won't think about how close you came to the edge again.

Yes. That was what she would do. That was the plan. And her plan would work, because Claire wanted and needed it to, and she'd worked hard for everything in her life and so she'd work hard for this, too.

Four hours later, the plane had touched down in Manchester amidst snow flurries, and Claire had trudged with a million other hollow-eyed passengers through Customs and Immigration, hauled her suitcase off the baggage carousel, and trudged some more to the rental car agency, where she'd filled seemingly endless paperwork despite all the forms she'd already filled out online, and was now in proud possession of the keys to a Honda Civic.

It was nine o'clock in the morning, and the sky outside was as gray as pewter, with mean little flakes of snow, not the fluffy, festive kind, drifting down on a muted grey landscape of concrete and leafless trees.

Claire dumped her bag in the trunk—or the boot, she supposed, someone in England would call it. Claire had always loved her godmother Ruth's English accent, and when she was a kid she'd quizzed Ruth on all the different British words. Pavement for sidewalk. Jumper for sweater. Rubber for eraser. The last one, of course, had caused eleven-year-old Claire to burst into muffled giggles of embarrassment and mirth. Ruth had just smiled, her eyes twinkling, sharing the admittedly immature joke.

Slowly, very conscious she was driving on the other side of the road, Claire pulled onto the road, and then followed signs for the M62 and York.

An hour and a half later, those mean little flakes of snow had turned thick and fluffy and white. They were beautiful, but her little car was not handling the snowy roads all that well. Growing up in Connecticut, Claire was used to snow. She'd driven through plenty of snowstorms and blizzards, but her car had been equipped with four-wheel drive and snow tires. In comparison the Civic felt like a toy car with tin wheels. Still she judged, hopefully with accuracy, that as long as the weather didn't get any worse, she'd make it to Ledstow.

It got worse.

The wipers were barely clearing the windshield of the heavy, wet flakes and the highway already had a blanket of several inches carpeting it. Outside the window, Claire glimpsed a blurry montage of rolling white fields bordered by drystone walls, she suspected would be beautiful if she could stop and actually look at them. If she wasn't consumed with not crashing the car or getting stuck in God Knows Where, England, with no working phone, no sleep, and very little suitable clothing.

It wasn't supposed to snow in England, but Claire acknowledged that she had not checked the weather in Yorkshire before she'd left. But still, wasn't England supposed to be mild and rainy?

The wheels of the Civic slid across the snow, and only by pumping the brake and gripping the wheel tightly was Claire able to keep from fishtailing across the highway.

This was not good. She was still about ten miles from Ledstow.

With sweat beading her forehead and her knuckles white on the steering wheel, Claire hunched forward, her gaze on the road. Each mile inched past; she wasn't even going twenty. Finally, after half an hour, she saw, through the now near-blizzard, a sign for Ledstow, and gratefully turned off the highway.

Onto a road that resembled a snow bank.

The road to Ledstow was narrow, with high hedges on

both sides and barely enough room for another car to pass. No one had plowed it, and the Civic skidded once again. The car spun slowly, as graceful as a ballet dancer, and ended up facing the wrong direction, the hood buried under a mini-avalanche of snow that had fallen from on top of the hedge, landing with a kind of gentle apology on the car, covering the windshield in whiteness.

Claire's breath came out in a rush and she leaned back against the seat, her heart pounding from the whole, surreal episode. She hadn't actually felt in danger, with all the softness surrounding her, but she had no idea what to do now. Her car was well and truly stuck, and there wasn't a person or building in sight.

After a moment, when her heart had stopped racing, she turned the car off and sat for a moment, the world silent around her, except for the gentle *thwack* of the snowflakes hitting the windows.

She was still two miles from Ledstow. Two miles, she decided, she could walk. She pulled the hood up on her coat, dug out her gloves and scarf from her bag, and squaring her shoulders, opened the door and stepped out into the storm.

NOAH BRADFORD STARED at the thick, white flakes drifting down outside his kitchen window and swore. The forecast had said the snow would hold off until Monday, but he should have known better than to trust the Met Office for an accurate update. The weather forecast changed every five minutes, and the weather in one Yorkshire dale could be different to the next, with each valley possessing its own microclimate. And Ledstow's microclimate, right now, was experiencing a blizzard.

Grimacing, he reached for the battered, waxed jacket he'd flung on a chair when he'd come in that morning from checking the animals in the barn, including several premature lambs, huddling under incubator lamps. He jammed his feet into his boots and his hat, with its leather earflaps, onto his head, and then headed out into the snow. He had two hundred sheep to move to the barn before they froze to death, buried under the snow, and he didn't intend to lose even one of them.

It wasn't easy work, even with Jake, his Border collie, helping to round the poor beasts up. Sheep were easily disoriented, and they milled about in circles, bleating piteously as the snow piled up on their backs and the cold froze their tails.

Slowly, laboriously, Noah herded the animals towards the wooden five-bar gate, and then down the dirt road, now barely visible under the mounded snow, towards the barn. Ayesgill Farm was situated just outside Lestow, with its fields running down to the narrow road that wound its way into the village. His grandfather had been the proud owner of two hundred acres, which Noah's father had reluctantly whittled down to one hundred and twenty-five before dying last year.

There wasn't much money in farming these days, but Noah was determined not to sell anymore off.

He counted the sheep as they jostled their way into the barn, and with his heart sinking, he saw he was two short. Two ewes he couldn't afford to lose.

Grimacing, he headed back to the fields with Jake at his side. The snow had turned icy, needling the exposed skin of his cheeks. He pulled his hat down lower on his head, tugged up his scarf over his mouth, and hunched his shoulders against the icy wind as he trudged through the snow that now slopped over the edge of his boots and soaked his thick wool socks. Enough snow had fallen for the huddled form of a ewe to be nearly impossible to find in the endless expanse of whiteness, but he still intended to try.

He figured the ewes hadn't come back with the others because they were stuck, either by a branch or in a gap in one of the drystone walls. He'd been out for an hour, his stomach growling from too many missed meals, his body frozen and soaked through, when he finally found the first, one hoof trapped by a fallen branch. He brushed the snow off her, everything in him clenching hard when he saw how frozen she was. He wasn't even sure if she was alive until she let out a pitiful mewling sound. He freed her hoof and trudged with her back to the barn, drying her off, and getting her warm before he headed back to look for the second. He didn't hold out much hope now; the temperatures were dropping, the snow having turned to freezing rain, but he couldn't leave her out there to freeze to death alone.

It took another hour of bleakly trudging the empty fields before he came to the ditch by the side of the road, the bottom filled with a foot of rainwater, and his poor ewe trapped there, shivering from both the snow and the icy water.

Noah swore, his voice carried away by the wind. Then he squared his shoulders and started down the steep side of the ditch, his boots slipping on the frozen, icy ground so he fell forward, landing at the bottom with an icy splash. He swore again.

"You had to come in here, I suppose?" he said, the ewe just bleating back. "I know, I know. It's effing freezing down here." He grabbed her by the scruff of her neck but she just bleated some more. "Damn it, you need to get back up there!" Talking to sheep was, Noah supposed, a hazard of spending most of his day with them. But this particular ewe didn't seem to be listening to him. He tried to haul her upwards, hoping she'd get the message, but she dug her hooves into the freezing water and resisted with all her might.

"Do you *want* to die?" Noah demanded in exasperation, and the ewe just looked balefully at him, the snow sleeting into her eyes.

Noah tried again, but with the angle of the side of the ditch and the foot of icy water and the snow, he knew he wasn't going to get anywhere without her cooperation—or some help. But there was no one to help, no one within miles, and by the time he reached a neighbor the ewe would most likely be dead.

"Damn it," he exclaimed, his words seeming to be absorbed by the snow, and then to his surprise he heard a voice, faint and tentative.

"Excuse me…"

He blinked up at the woman who had appeared like an angel over the side of the ditch, her long, dark hair dusted with snowflakes, her cheeks bright scarlet from the cold.

She wore a hat, scarf, and parka but she was still shivering as she asked, "Do you need any help?"

CHAPTER TWO

CLAIRE HAD BEEN trudging along the side of the road for close to an hour when she'd heard a man swearing. She stopped, shocked by how close he sounded, and how angry. Who on earth was out here in this weather, having an argument with someone?

Then his tone changed from angry to defeated and even despairing, and even though eight years as a New Yorker told her to be careful of crazies, she clambered up the side of the ditch from where she'd heard the voice and peeked over.

The man was talking to a sheep.

Okay, that was a new one. She watched as he wrestled the poor beast for a moment, and realized the animal was stuck in the ditch, refusing to move upwards, towards safety. And even though she didn't know the first thing about sheep or farmers or anything about this situation she offered to help.

The man swung towards her, and Claire couldn't tell a thing from his expression, what with his hat jammed low on his head, and his scarf drawn over his mouth. She couldn't tell much about the man at all, except that he was tall and strong-looking—although clearly not strong enough to shift a reluctant sheep on his own.

"Are you serious?" he asked.

His voice sounded gruff, yet with a pleasant Yorkshire burr, and she blinked back the snow that had become very cold and very wet, needling any bit of exposed skin.

"Yes—"

"Then come here and you can push her backside."

Claire eyed the foot or so of icy, dirty water that pooled in the bottom of the ditch and realized why the man had asked if she were serious.

Gingerly she took a step down the side of the ditch. The ground was icy and slick and if she wasn't careful, she'd end up on her backside, as stuck as the poor sheep. Also, she was wearing her Prada leather boots. She'd bought them as treat for herself and they now looked to become totally ruined.

The sheep bleated again, and resolutely Claire continued down the steep side of the ditch. She couldn't leave the poor animal to freeze to death. She tried to navigate the freezing water pooling in the ditch by stepping on bits of frozen mud and grass, but she quickly saw that this was not the type of endeavor she could be squeamish about. Grimly, she stepped into the water and waded through it towards the sheep, sucking in a hard breath as water seeped into her boots and the cold into her very bones.

"Push her up the backside," the man instructed and Claire glanced at the sheep's rear with ill-concealed distaste.

Sheep, she realized, were dirty animals. Bits of dirt and poo were stuck on the sheep's raggedy wool and even with her gloves on, she really didn't want to touch any of it.

"Are you going to do it or not?" The man asked in exasperation.

With a deep breath and a nod Claire planted her two hands on the animal's rear and shoved.

The man, meanwhile, had grabbed the sheep around the middle and was hauling her towards him. The sheep bleated piteously, as if it were being murdered, and Claire saw that its legs were stuck in the frozen mud.

"Wait," she called. "The sheep—its legs—"

With a curse under his breath, the man waded into the water next to her and plunged one arm down, working at the mud around the sheep's hoof. Claire stood there, her feet soaked, her boots ruined, and probably in danger of contracting hypothermia. Right now coming to Yorkshire felt like a very bad idea.

The man straightened, one arm soaked to the shoulder, and gave her a terse nod. "Let's try again."

Claire gave enough push. The man pulled, and thankfully, with an awful sucking sound, the sheep's hooves came out of the mud. The animal hurtled forward so that the man fell flat on his back, his breath coming out in a single *oof,* his arms still around the wet and muddy sheep, his Border collie licking his face.

Claire let out a single bubble of laughter at the sight of

him embracing the sheep and then clapped her hand over her mouth. The man glanced at her, and she thought she saw amusement light his whiskey-brown eyes. His eyes were about the only thing she could see of him.

"Right, then." He scrambled to a standing position, one hand still on the scruff of the sheep's neck, the dog by his heels. "Need a hand?" He stretched a hand out which Claire grabbed gratefully. She clambered up the ditch alongside him, until they were all standing, man, woman, dog, and sheep, at the edge of a snowy field without a house or building in sight.

"Thank you," he said, his voice gruff. "I couldn't have got her out on my own." He nodded towards her boots. "You're soaked."

"Yes." Claire glanced down at her ruined boots with a sigh. So much for Prada.

"You're not from around here," he remarked and she gave a little laugh.

"Definitely not. Actually, my car is stuck in a snow bank and I was walking to Ledstow. I'm staying at Holly Cottage—you wouldn't happen to know it?"

"It's near my farm," the man answered with a nod. "I can take you there, if you like, after I deal with her." He nodded towards the sheep, and Claire gave him a grateful smile. She was exhausted, dirty, and wet, and the thought of actually reaching her destination, and a bed she could lie down in, sounded like heaven.

"Thanks so much—"

"We ought to get going before the snow gets any worse," he said, and set off. Claire followed him across the field, the wet snow slopping into her boots and stinging her face.

Fifteen minutes later they approach a farm, with two stone barns and a low, rambling whitewashed farmhouse making three sides of a square. The man headed into the largest barn with the sheep, and Claire hesitated on the threshold as she watched him dry the animal, as tender now as a mother with her child. He set the beast along with the others and then turned back to her.

"It's another fifteen minutes to Holly Cottage, and you're soaking wet. You ought to come in and dry off, have a cup of tea before we set off again. You don't want to get hypothermia."

"No..." Claire agreed slowly, because while she saw the sense in his plan, he was a stranger and she was in the middle of nowhere. She didn't even have the security blanket of a working cell phone.

But this was Yorkshire, not New York, and she'd seen this man take care of a sheep as if it were his own child. She felt, instinctively, that she could trust him. Besides, she was utterly freezing.

He clearly took her silence for agreement for he beckoned her forward. "Come on, then," he said, and started across the field, the Border collie trotting beside him.

Claire followed, picking her away across the snow-covered farmyard to the house. The man stooped to enter the low doorway with its ancient, blackened lintel, and Claire stepped inside behind him, the warmth of the cozy, cluttered kitchen enveloping her like a much needed blanket.

The man shucked off his wet clothes and boots and after a second's pause Claire did the same, draping her sopping coat over a chair and tugging down the zipper on her ruined boots.

"I'll get you some dry socks," the man said, and then stuck out a hand. "I'm Noah Bradford, by the way."

Claire looked up, one hand already stretched out towards his, and felt everything in her jolt with surprise and awareness.

Noah Bradford was *hot*.

She swallowed audibly as his huge, callused hand enclosed hers, and tried to yank her gaze away from his face with those warm brown eyes she'd seen above his scarf, and the chiseled jaw she hadn't. He had a shock of brown hair to go with the eyes, a surprisingly mobile mouth, and a *body*...

Her gaze had dropped, seemingly of its own accord, to Noah Bradford's well-defined chest. His thermal shirt clung to his pecs, and when she dropped her gaze lower she saw how his wet jeans molded to his thighs and butt.

She'd assumed, underneath all those protective layers, Noah Bradford was an older man, craggy and haggard, the kind of sheep farmer who ate with his boots on and slept in his suspenders.

Not… this.

"Claire Lindell," she murmured and Noah released her hand and walked over to the huge, battered Aga cooking range that took up nearly a whole wall in the low-ceilinged kitchen. He hefted a large brass kettle from its top and filled it from the tap over a deep, stone sink, a window above it overlooking the farmyard now covered in snow.

Claire's gaze moved around the room, from the scarred, pine table piled high with newspapers, paperwork, and dirty dishes. Mugs of half-drunk tea or coffee littered nearly every surface. Clothes, none looking too clean, hung over the railing of the Aga, and more were heaped on the floor, next to a jumble of muddy boots.

Noah had turned from the stove and now caught sight of Claire staring at all the mess. He lifted one shoulder in a shrug of apology.

"Sorry. The place is a tip."

"A… tip?"

His mouth curved in a way that made things pop low in Claire's belly. "Sorry, a mess. You're American." She nodded, although it hadn't been a question.

"From New York."

"City?" he clarified, and she nodded. She couldn't tell if she was imagining it, but it almost seemed as if Noah Bradford didn't like that fact. His mouth tightened and he nodded towards her feet. "I'll get you those socks. You can hang up your wet things on the stove. Just shove my kit onto the floor. It's all dirty."

He disappeared through another doorway and gingerly Claire moved through the room, towards the welcoming heat of the Aga.

She pushed Noah's things aside, not quite willing to toss them onto the floor as he'd suggested, and hung up her coat, scarf, and gloves. The heat rolled out from the huge cooking range, making the room cozily warm, despite all the mess. Part of her itched to dump a few dishes into the sink, tidy the papers into neat piles.

Stupid, stupid impulse. She might be borderline OCD but she didn't need to try to fix someone else's life, not even a little bit. She knew where that went, and it was nowhere good.

She could hear Noah returning, the steady tread of his feet, and she turned from the Aga as he came through the door. He'd changed into dry clothes and held a pair of thick, wool socks in his hands. He tossed them to her from across the room, and Claire caught them instinctively.

"Put those on. You can't have wet feet."

Obediently, she took off her soaking socks and hung them up on the railing before putting on the thick ones Noah had tossed her. They didn't go exactly well with skinny jeans, but they were warm and dry, if a little itchy.

The kettle started to shrill and Noah moved past her, his arm brushing her shoulder as he reached across her for the kettle. Hurriedly, Claire backed up a few steps, out of the way. The whole experience felt incredibly surreal.

"So what's an American, and a New Yorker at that, doing in Yorkshire?" Noah asked as he plunked two tea bags in chipped, ceramic mugs and poured boiling water on top.

"Having Christmas by myself."

He arched an eyebrow, and too late Claire realized how pathetic it sounded.

"I mean," she explained awkwardly, "that's what I want. A quiet Christmas, with nobody around." Now she sounded like Scrooge.

"Sounds good to me." He stared at her rather broodingly, seeming disinclined to ask any more questions, which suited Claire fine. She wasn't inclined to explain why she wanted to be four thousand miles away from family, eating a Christmas dinner for one, probably a pizza.

Noah tossed the tea bags into the sink, where they landed with a wet thud. He poured milk into the mugs and then reached for a chipped sugar bowl, arching an eyebrow in Claire's direction as he hefted the spoon.

"Yes, please," she said, thinking she could use a sugar hit, and he dumped two heaping teaspoonfuls of granules into each of their mugs and stirred. Wow. That was a lot of sugar.

He handed her a mug, wrapping one lean, brown hand around his own as he braced a hip against the sink. Claire felt an impulse to make small talk, which she resisted. Noah Bradford clearly wasn't one for pleasantries, and she was feeling too tired and overwhelmed to do more than sip the syrupy-sweet tea.

"So your car," Noah said after a moment. "It's stuck on the high road?"

"The road from the highway, yes," Claire answered. "I skidded and plowed right into a snow bank."

Noah glanced out the kitchen window, the icy rain still sheeting down. "There's no point getting it out until this all stops," he said with a nod to the rain. "And the roads are gritted. But we'll fetch your stuff."

"Thank you—"

He drained his mug and set it, unsurprisingly, on the countertop, along with half a dozen others that had been left and forgotten. Claire took another sip of hers; she'd barely touched it, but Noah seemed ready to go.

The Border collie stirred from his place by the Aga as Noah reached for his waxed jacket and shrugged it on. Claire put her tea down and started putting her still-damp things back on.

A few moments later they were back outside with the wind blowing the rain into their eyes. Claire followed Noah over to a battered Land Rover; he opened the passenger door and she climbed in, breathing in the scent of dog and sheep and man, not an unpleasant combination of aromas.

Noah got in the driver seat and slammed the door before wiping the water from his eyes. "Not pretty out there," he said, and Claire murmured an agreement.

Then he started the car and drove away from the farm, down a long, curving, snow-covered lane.

CHAPTER THREE

NOAH SLID A sideways glance at Claire Lindell and suppressed the flare of curiosity he felt about this woman, a fish out of water in a Yorkshire farming village. She wore jeans and a sweater, but even he could tell they were both expensive. Her long, dark hair framed a pale, oval face with large gray eyes and a surprisingly full mouth. When she'd taken off all her wet things he'd felt a kick of attraction low in his belly that had taken him by surprise. That was the last thing he needed, especially for a woman whose boots looked to cost more than his council tax.

He focused back on the road, the snow and rain flying right into the windshield as he turned onto the narrow road that connected Ledstow to the highway. After about five minutes of careful driving, he saw a car with its front buried in the hedge, the rest of it already covered in freshly fallen snow.

"Did you lock it?" he asked, and Claire blinked at him, as startled as a rabbit caught in the headlight of his Rover.

"Yes—"

He held out his hand. "I'll get your things and put them

in here," he explained and he could tell she was a little wary of his offer. Maybe they did things differently in America.

"Okay," she said after a moment, and fished her keys from the pocket of her parka. "Thank you," she added, an afterthought, and he nodded and then stepped outside into the storm. No need to get cozy with Claire Lindell.

He unlocked the car and grabbed her handbag, a canvas hold-all that looked like it was full of papers. Her suitcase was Gucci, and even he recognized that name. So his suspicions had been on the money, literally. She was rich. A rich, city girl.

And he steered clear of rich city girls.

He dumped the bags in the back of the Land Rover and got back in the driver's seat. Claire was shivering, even though he'd left the engine running and the heat on. Her jeans, he realized, were soaked. Should he have offered to lend her some clothes, back at his place? That seemed a little familiar, and he sensed that just driving her to her car had been pushing boundaries with this woman. Although she'd been perfectly polite, she exuded a kind of brittle formality; her shoulders were set stiffly, her posture perfect. Maybe she was worried he was some kind of serial killer, or maybe she was just prissy.

Either way, she'd be out of his life in ten minutes.

"Holly Cottage," he said, and turned the Rover around, back towards Ledstow.

They drove in silence, the only sound the crunch of the

tires on snow. Against his better judgment, Noah snuck another glance at his passenger. She was beautiful, in a quiet, poised sort of way. She held herself very still and erect, and yet there was something vulnerable and even sad about the curve of her cheek, the sweep of her lashes.

Noah grimaced at his fanciful thoughts. His brother David used to tease him about the red squirrels and baby sparrows he'd nursed back to health as a kid on the farm. He'd been a sucker for a sad face, and that was what had got him in so much trouble. He didn't want to know Claire Lindell's story, sad or not, and yet as he turned down the road that led to Holly Cottage he asked,

"So, what brought you to Ledstow?"

A hesitation; he felt it. She didn't want to tell him anything? Fine. He didn't want to know.

"My godmother owns Holly Cottage," she finally said, and he heard how crisp and cultured her voice sounded.

"Ruth Carrington is your godmother?"

She glanced at him, gray eyes wide. "You know her?"

"Ledstow is a small place."

"Of course."

"Holly Cottage abuts Ayesgill Farm," he explained. "I've had a few sheep wandering into her garden."

Her eyes widened a fraction more, and she clearly had no response.

"Don't worry," Noah hastened to assure her. "They're going to stay in the barn as long as this snow keeps up."

"Is this... normal? This much snow?"

He shrugged. "This is Yorkshire."

They didn't speak again until he'd pulled to a stop in front of Holly Cottage; it was a small place, made of golden Yorkshire stone, with a bay window and a peaked roof. Claire stared at it without expression, and Noah wondered if the place wasn't grand enough for the likes of her.

Not a charitable or fair thought, but he wondered all the same.

"I'll just get the key," she murmured and Noah opened the door to the Land Rover.

"There's one under the flower pot," he said and she swung a startled gaze towards him. He shrugged again. "Ruth has me watch over the place when she's not around. She didn't tell me you were coming, though."

"It was last minute," Claire said.

Noah felt another flicker of curiosity. Claire Lindell looked like the kind of woman whose Christmas plans would be settled in July; maybe a cruise to the Caribbean or a weekend in Paris. Expensive holidays, spas and five-star hotels and restaurants. Not a poky cottage in an even pokier village in the middle of Yorkshire, all on her own.

What had happened to make Claire take off into isolation at the last minute?

He wouldn't ask.

He took the key from under the flowerpot and opened the front door to the cottage. Claire followed behind him, clutching her bag to her chest.

"I can show you how to put the heat on if you like," he offered, because the cottage was freezing and he doubted there was any hot water.

"Thank you," she murmured and Noah moved through the sitting room with its inglenook fireplace to the tiny kitchen in the back, everything cozy and neat as Ruth liked, with a view of his own sheep fields stretching to a snowy horizon.

Quickly, he went through the basics of the heating system, switching on the hot water immersion heater. "You can have a bath in an hour or so," he told her, "but the shower is electric and runs anytime."

A slight blush pinkened her cheeks and an image, unbidden and definitely unwanted, popped into his head of Claire Lindell in the bath, all that creamy skin on show, with nothing covering her but a few strategically placed bubbles.

Good Lord. Noah passed a hand over his face, embarrassed by how quickly the image had come into his head, and how much it had affected him. Clearly his social life was lacking; he couldn't even remember the last time he'd been with a woman. Over a year ago, at least; he'd had a few unmemorable one-night stands when he'd gone on business to York or Newcastle. He'd never wanted to get involved with someone from Ledstow, even if there had been the opportunity. Never wanted to have his past dragged out like so much battered baggage, a hell of a lot different from

Claire's Gucci suitcases.

"So you're good?" he asked Claire and she nodded jerkily.

"Is there a shop in the village?"

"A post office that sells a few basics, milk and bread mainly," Noah answered. He realized that without the use of her car, Claire Lindell was essentially stranded with no food. Just in case, he checked Ruth's fridge, but efficient as ever, she'd cleared it out in preparation for Claire's arrival. "You need food," he said, a statement, and she gave a kind of helpless shrug.

"I can run you into Ripon, to the supermarket," he offered, and he couldn't tell if the swirl of feeling in his gut was anticipation or dread. He'd wanted to rid himself of Claire Lindell, with her sad eyes and expensive clothes, but he also had an idiotic urge to help her, maybe even make her smile. As if that was going to happen. "It's about fifteen minutes," he added, and watched as she nibbled her lip, clearly uncertain about whether to accept his request. Was she worried he was going to make a move? Or was his battered Land Rover smelling of sheep not good enough for her?

With a slight edge to his voice he continued, "Or you can live on toast and beans. It works for me."

She stared at him for a moment, startled and clearly trying to judge his mood, and Noah realized that he'd sounded a little pissy.

Because he didn't like rich girls with sad eyes who

couldn't decide if he was good enough for them. And there was his baggage, dragging behind him, weighing him down.

"Whatever you like," he said, and turned away.

"Sorry, I'm just really tired and jet-lagged," she said and guilt twisted inside him. He was being an ass, and it had nothing to do with Claire Lindell. "I'd be very grateful if you could drive me into town," she added. "But could it be a little later? I want to change and shower…"

More images popped into his head, of a body slick with water and soap. Noah nodded tersely.

"No worries. I'll swing back in a couple of hours, when I've checked on the animals."

"That would be great."

He nodded again and with no reason to stay any longer, he headed for the front door. "See you in a bit," he said, and was gone.

CLAIRE CLOSED THE door behind Noah Bradford and let out a rush of breath. Tension knotted between her shoulders and exhaustion was crashing over her in a wave, making her sway where she stood. The endless flight, followed by an endless drive. The snow, the storm, the sheep…

And Noah Bradford.

He'd been so helpful and even friendly, in his gruff, farmer's way, but just before he'd left she'd felt something almost like animosity coming from him. It had given her pause, but she needed food and she was too tired to untangle any kind of emotional complexity. She'd spent too much of her life already doing exactly that with a man; months and months of analyzing every easy smile he'd given her, every seemingly careless touch of her hand, wondering if she dared read anything into it, or if she even wanted to.

She couldn't do that anymore. Briefly she rested her head against the door, too tired even to move. She'd made it through a month of school with her head held high, having no idea if she'd be called into the Headmistress's office and given her notice for improper behavior. Having no idea if she'd been the architect of her life's destruction or not. She'd made it through concerts and finals and an awful conversation with her mother, punctuated by long, frosty silences and disappointed sighs, and then through the flight and the drive and even putting her hands on a sheep's backside and shoving...

A little hiccup of near-hysterical laughter bubbled up inside her. *I'm too tired*, she thought, *and too empty. I need to sleep for a hundred hours. I need a glass—or even a bottle—of wine...*

But first a shower, and fresh clothes, and maybe a power nap. She'd buy food for the week, she'd thank Noah Bradford for his kindness, and then she'd call the British equivalent of AAA to get her car out of the snow bank, and she'd never see the unsettling sheep farmer again.

With all those resolutions wearily passed, Claire headed

upstairs.

Two hours later a distant, steady knocking woke her up slowly from the dead sleep she'd fallen into, still wrapped in a towel, her hair damp from the shower she'd stayed in for twenty minutes until she'd finally started to feel warm.

She blinked fuzzily, gazing wildly around the unfamiliar room until her gaze settled on a photo of Ruth Carrington with Claire's mother, both college girls at Vassar, and she remembered where she was. She let out a shaky breath and then jumped up from the bed, grabbing the thick, fleece bathrobe that hung from the bathroom door. She pushed her hands into the sleeves and tied the sash as tightly as she could before she ran downstairs and opened the front door to Noah Bradford.

He looked exactly the same, wearing a battered wax jacket and jeans, his eyes widening slightly as he took in the sight of her.

Claire knew she must look a mess. She could feel dried drool on her cheek, and her hair had dried as she'd slept, and was now sticking out in about sixteen different directions. And she was wearing a bathrobe.

"Sorry, sorry," she hurried to explain, fighting a flush that threatened to cover her from head to toe. "I fell asleep."

"I gathered that," Noah answered, his tone so dry that Claire surprised herself by smiling.

And then Noah surprised her by noticing and smiling back, his eyes crinkling as his mouth kicked up at the corner and Claire felt a jolt of awareness like a blast of heat she hadn't expected, warming her all the way through.

Oh, no. She could not go there. Would not. Not when she was so hurting and unhappy, her heart still aching from far too many bitter and shaming memories.

"Let me just get dressed," she mumbled and headed upstairs.

Back in Ruth's bedroom, she yanked on a pair of fresh jeans and another cashmere sweater, pushed her feet into sneakers, and then grabbed her bag still filled with unmarked final exams. She dumped them out on the bed, wincing at the confetti of bluebooks, with the neat cursive all the girls at Stirling were required to master, that fluttered down on the unmade bed. Turning away from the mess, she hurried downstairs.

Noah had come inside the cottage's little slate-tiled foyer and stood there, his face expressionless, his hands tucked deep inside the pockets of his jacket. His expression didn't change as he caught sight of her, but Claire still felt something, some kind of discomfort or awkwardness. Then she caught sight of herself in the little hall mirror and let out a shaky laugh. She'd forgotten to brush her hair, and it looked like a complete bird's nest.

Quickly she combed her fingers through it and then grabbed an elastic band from her bag and pulled her hair into a haphazard ponytail. "Sorry for the wait," she said, and Noah just shrugged her apology aside before heading back outside.

It had stopped snowing while she'd been sleeping, and the world was pristine and white, the air crisp and cold. It was only about three o'clock in the afternoon, but already the sky was turning a pale violet at its edges, like a bruise, and long shadows lay across the snowy fields.

"It gets dark early," Claire said, the words immediately sounding inane, and Noah just nodded. She felt keyed up and a little exposed; he'd seen her in her bathrobe, after all. Small talk, she hoped, might help, might make sense of this strange, surreal situation. "Are you from around here?" she asked.

"Yes."

It was, Claire decided, a rather abrupt answer. As she'd suspected before, Noah Bradford was not inclined to pleasantries. Well, fine. She hadn't come to Yorkshire to make friends.

She turned and stared out the window; they had driven down the narrow road from Holly Cottage and were now coming into the village proper, which looked to be no more than a narrow street of terraced houses and barn conversions, a tiny post office shop in the middle, with a bow window and blackened beams. Noah drove out the other side of the village and then in silence for several miles until they arrived at civilization: a sign announcing the Historic Market Town of Ripon, the spire of a cathedral in the distance, and on the outskirts, a few big-box stores including a large supermarket called Sainsbury's.

Once more murmuring her thanks, Claire slipped out of the Land Rover as soon as Noah had parked the car. There was something unsettling and weirdly intimate about food shopping with a man, almost as if they were a couple, which of course they were not.

She pushed the cart through the aisles with Noah trailing after her, hands shoved in his pockets, as she took in the unfamiliar food items—Cornish pasties, sausage rolls—mixed with the familiar boxes of cereal and loaves of bread.

She felt acutely self-conscious as she selected a single box of muesli, a tub of plain yogurt, a pint of skimmed milk. She bought a couple of ready meals-for-one, as she'd never been much of a cook, and even though part of her longed to be able to roll pastry and dust flour, to feel motherly and wifely and the rest of it, she stayed away from the baking aisle, from the roast chickens and joints of beef, the trappings of family life. That kind of instinct had led her nowhere good.

She paused at the wine aisle, longing to take a bottle, but feeling like she'd look pathetic, buying wine to drink on her own at Holly Cottage. Never go food shopping with a stranger, she decided, and she was just about to push past the alcohol when Noah's cellphone trilled and she heard him say tersely,

"Dani?"

She stilled, because there had been a kind of guarded familiarity in his voice, a tone that had made her feel guiltily curious. Who was Dani—or Danny? Boy or girl?

She couldn't tell because Dani, whoever he or she was, was speaking, and Noah was silent, although Claire didn't think she was being fanciful in thinking that his silence was tense, even ominous.

"What do you mean, you can't have her?" he asked finally, his voice low and furious. "She's not a *cat*, for—" He bit off whatever oath he'd been going to make, turning his back on Claire, his phone clenched to his ear.

Claire picked up a box of cereal bars from a tottering pile at the end of an aisle and made a big show of intently studying the ingredients. Noah had taken a few steps away, to stand by the deli counter, his shoulders hunched, his chin tucked in, and yet she could still hear his voice.

"It's Christmas, Dani. It's an important holiday for a— no, I don't have plans." Out of the corner of her eye Claire saw Noah rake a hand through his hair, his fingers clenching on the disheveled strands, before he dropped it to hang wearily by his side. "What I mean is," he continued after a moment, his voice careful, "that Molly will want to be with you, will be expecting a proper—" Another silence, taut with suppressed tension. Although his back was to her, Claire thought she could imagine the look on Noah's face. The tension she'd see bunching his jaw, narrowing his eyes.

He straightened, his shoulders rigid. "Of course she can stay with me." Anther silence. "Tonight?" The one word rose incredulously, loudly enough for customers nearby to glance at him in both curiosity and disapproval. "Fine," he bit out. "Fine. I'll be home in an hour."

He disconnected the call and thrust the phone into the pocket of his jacket, standing still for a moment, his body practically thrumming with anger. Then he turned sharply on his heel and walked back to Claire.

She put down the box of cereal bars, trying to keep her face pleasantly neutral, as if she hadn't heard a word of his phone conversation.

Noah stared at her for a moment, clearly struggling to contain his anger, and then finally he forced out, "Looks like I need to do a bit of food shopping as well. I'll just go get a trolley." And without waiting for a reply, he turned and walked away.

CHAPTER FOUR

N OAH FLEXED HIS hands, trying to suppress the urge to hit something. Typical Dani, to wait until the last minute to arrange childcare for their daughter. Typical of her to think only of herself, and not what Molly needed or wanted. Not what an eight-year-old would feel, knowing she was being shunted off for Christmas because her flake of a mother had decided she wanted to go to the Caribbean with her boyfriend of the month, instead of spending the holiday at home with her daughter.

Noah knew his thoughts were uncharitable, if not precisely unfair, and he'd always tried to keep himself from thinking or speaking negatively of Dani, because he knew it didn't help anyone: not Dani, who was helpless and flighty and not Molly, who naturally loved her mother, and not him, who knew the old anger still burned in his chest, nine years after it had all happened.

He took a steadying breath as he reached for a trolley. He needed to think about Molly now. Briefly, he thought of Claire, of that clear, wide-eyed gaze she'd given him as he'd stood there, trying not to let out a stream of swear words.

She must think he was mad, Noah thought ruefully, and decided that was no bad thing. He still felt a flicker of attraction for her, and even that was too much. Even now he could picture her in her bathrobe, her cheeks flushed, her hair a mess, the shadowy valley between her breasts just visible when she'd opened the door in just a dressing gown.

Resolutely, he banished the image and began to push the trolley through the supermarket, grabbing things at random. Bananas, oranges, apples. What did an eight-year-old girl like to eat? He didn't know, because his visits with Molly had always been Saturday afternoons spent in York, going to the cinema or the Railway Museum, shopping in the Shambles, and then finishing with dinner at McDonalds. The classic divorced dad line-up, although he and Dani had never actually got around to getting married.

But now Dani wanted him to have Molly at his house for four whole days... hell, was it even legal? What if he lost his custody rights because he'd violated the terms of their arrangement?

A cold sweat prickled between his shoulder blades and he grabbed a couple of boxes of sugary cereal and tossed them into the trolley. He'd phone his solicitor as soon as he'd dropped Claire off. He couldn't risk jeopardizing his custody agreement, not even for Dani. But he knew it wouldn't really matter what the man said, because he couldn't say no to Dani, and he certainly wouldn't let his daughter down. She had nowhere else to go; Dani's friends weren't exactly maternal, and her parents had decided, despite their heartfelt pleas to the court years ago, that they'd prefer to pretend their granddaughter didn't exist.

So Molly would be with him. He'd have his daughter to himself for four whole days… a prospect that filled him with both elation and terror.

He found Claire at the checkout; she'd added two bottles of wine to her trolley and was perusing the Sainsbury's Home Magazine by the till, a picture of a burnished turkey surrounded by golden roasted potatoes on its cover.

She glanced up and saw him, looking almost guilty as she stuffed the magazine back in the rack, almost as if he'd caught her looking at porn. Then her gaze caught sight of his trolley, overflowing with every conceivable food item, and her mouth parted slightly in surprise.

Noah glanced down at the boxes of cereal, the dozen apples, the three bunches of bananas. The loaves of bread and packs of chicken breasts, bags of pasta and rice, and jars of sauces. All right, so he'd gone a bit overboard. But he knew his cupboards were empty; he actually knew how to cook, but he rarely had the time or inclination to whip up a meal for one.

"Expecting company?" she asked.

Before he could help himself, he answered, "Yeah. My daughter."

Her gaze widened but she didn't reply, just started helping him put it all on the conveyor belt. Her own things, he saw, were already bagged and paid for, everything returned neatly to her trolley.

Panic was starting to sour his gut and chill his mind as he began to bag all the food he was buying. Dani had said she'd bring Molly over tonight, and his house was a complete tip. He wasn't even sure if he had clean sheets. And the animals needed tending, and his television didn't even work, and *shit*. Four days. What was he going to do?

"Breathe," Claire murmured, and put the marshmallows he'd been holding into the bag as he stared blankly into space. "It'll be okay."

"She's never stayed with me before," he explained tersely, and even that was just the tip of the iceberg of his sad and tired history. He closed his eyes briefly, then snapped them open and with his jaw tight, he began to lob the food into the bag.

CLAIRE COVERTLY WATCHED Noah as she helped him bag the groceries, wondering just what the history between him and his ex was. She had no right to ask or even wonder, and she shouldn't even want to. Good Lord, if Noah Bradford having a daughter wasn't the biggest red flag that had ever been waved in front of her.

Look, a man with a daughter, a man you're attracted to, who would make a good husband, is a good father. Here's your happily-ever-after, Claire, all neatly packaged and tied with a bow. Go for it.

No, she would not be drinking that Kool-Aid again. Not in a million years. And in any case, they'd known each other for about five minutes. She was ridiculous to be *thinking* of anything with Noah Bradford, even in the negative. He was a helpful stranger, nothing more.

Noah paid for his groceries, his expression grim, and they walked out in silence back to the Land Rover. Claire thought she could piece enough of the story together from Noah's phone call; his ex had asked him to take care of their daughter unexpectedly, for Christmas. His terse words echoed through her mind. *'It's Christmas, Dani. It's an important holiday. Of course she can stay with me.'*

Noah Bradford cared about his daughter, even if he'd said he didn't see her all that much.

Noah loaded all their bags into the back of the Land Rover, and Claire climbed into the passenger seat. It was all so weirdly, cozily domestic. And yet not.

She glanced around the car, noticing the travel cup that had the dregs of what looked like very old coffee still in it, as well as something called malt loaf with its packaging torn open and then wrapped haphazardly back up, stuffed next to the travel cup. Maps, boots, gloves, and a coil of rope littered the backseat. She heard the back slam and then Noah climbed in next to her, smelling cold and clean, his expression still grim and tense as he glanced at the clock on the dash.

"Are you in a hurry?" she asked, knowing that he was, and he gave a brief nod.

"My daughter's being dropped off in about an hour." Claire thought of the mess of his kitchen, and couldn't quite keep from wincing. Noah noticed and let out a laugh that managed to sound both wry and despairing. "I know. I'm not exactly ready."

"I could help you," Claire said, the words out of her mouth before they'd truly formed in her head. *No, Claire. You don't want to do that. You can't want to do that.*

And yet, helplessly, she did.

Noah slid her a wary glance, as if trying to assess the sincerity of her offer. "You don't have to do that," he said gruffly, and Claire told herself to accept the rebuff, to shrug and say something meaningless, but instead more words came, words she hadn't meant to say, to mean.

"I don't mind. You've certainly helped me out today. And frankly, I think you need it. Your kitchen was a complete mess."

He let another laugh, this one sounding genuine. "Thanks for the honesty."

"My pleasure."

He didn't reply, and Claire waited, willing herself not to beg. *Say yes. Want me. Need me.*

She turned towards the window, hating that she'd fallen into her old pattern less than twenty-four or even twelve hours of getting off the plane. Did desperate men with

41

daughters *look* for her?

No, you just have a homing instinct for them.

"Well, if you don't mind," Noah finally said, his gaze straight ahead on the snowy road. He sounded reluctant, like he didn't want to need her help, but knew he really did.

And ruthlessly, resolutely, Claire popped the entirely inappropriate bubble of excitement and happiness that rose inside her at the thought.

Fine, you can clean his kitchen, repay the debt, and then you can go home and never see Noah Bradford again.

She was such a pathetic idiot.

He let her off at Holly Cottage, and Claire dumped her food in the fridge before she climbed back into the Land Rover and headed for Ayesgill Farm.

"I'll get your car tomorrow," Noah said as they drove back down the lane. "It should be all right overnight. Not many people will be on the road."

She nodded, still bemused and more than a little alarmed at how quickly their lives had become entwined. He was getting her car. She was cleaning his kitchen. Why didn't they just move in together?

This is just payback. A favor for a favor. It doesn't have to be a big deal. She'd help him clean and then she'd go back to Holly Cottage, open a bottle of wine, pop a meal in the microwave, grade a few exams. Fun, fun, fun.

Night had fallen by the time Noah pulled into the farmyard. Used to the orange electric glow of the urban night, Claire was unprepared for the utter darkness that engulfed her as she stepped out of the Land Rover. Blackness stretched in every direction, broken only by the glow of a single lamp inside the farmhouse, and the diamond pinpricks of stars above.

She tilted her head and gazed at all those stars; she didn't think she'd ever seen so many before in her life. She took a deep breath of cold, crisp air that came out in a surprised rush as she felt Noah's hands close around her shoulders.

She lost her balance and swayed into him, her back hitting his chest, her butt curving into his thighs. Noah's hands tightened on her shoulders and for a moment it felt as if her heart were suspended in her chest before going into free fall.

Noah steadied her, moving her away from him, before he dropped his hands from her shoulders. "Sorry," he muttered. "I didn't see you there."

"Sorry," Claire mumbled back.

Her heart started beating wildly. Stupid heart. Stupid in so many ways. She felt clumsy and thick-fingered as she went around helping with the bags and bringing them into the house. She could feel how flushed she was, and hoped Noah didn't notice.

Neither spoke as they transferred all the shopping to his kitchen, and by the time they were both inside with their coats and hats and scarves off, Claire had thankfully regained most of her composure.

"I'll make a start on the kitchen," she offered. "If you want to do the upstairs." He nodded, pointed out the ancient-looking cleaning spray underneath the sink, and then disappeared through the low doorway to the sitting room.

Claire took a deep breath, let it out slowly. Okay. She was here, and she was going to clean. She took all the dirty dishes to the sink, and then emptied the half-full dishwasher. She suspected Noah had just been taking the clean dishes out only as he needed them. She reloaded the dishwasher and then started making piles. She was a compulsive organizer, and she couldn't not put the papers scattered across the scarred pine table into some kind of order. Newspapers went in the recycling bin; bills went on top of the Welsh dresser that held a lot of dusty Wedgewood china.

As she cleaned, Claire couldn't help but notice that messy as it was, this was not the typical bachelor pad. The dresser full of china, the drawers of tarnished sterling silver, another stuffed full of papers that looked like they went back twenty years. This was, she believed, Noah's childhood home, and that made her all the more curious about him. Had he taken on the family farm? Where were his parents? Did he have brothers or sisters?

They were all questions she had no intention of asking.

She sprayed down the counters and mopped the floor, wondering if she should be so bold as to start getting a meal together for Noah and his daughter. No, that would be presumptuous. Pathetic, too, and cringingly embarrassing, if he thought she wanted to be invited, included.

Which of course she didn't. Besides, she couldn't cook

all that well, even though she liked the idea of it, of providing a meal for people she loved.

Claire pushed away memories of sitting at another table, one made of chrome and glass, doling out green bean casserole to Mark and Brianna. Feeling the fragile bubble of happiness inside her, thinking it was real, that she was actually a part of something.

She would not go down that road again, not even an inch, which meant she needed to leave. Now.

Noah came into the room, doing a double take at the sight of the clean kitchen. "Wow, that's quite impressive. It's only been twenty minutes."

She shrugged. "I kind of like cleaning."

"That's lucky for me."

"Is there anything else I can help with?" Not the question she should have been asking if she really intended to leave as soon as possible.

Noah ran a hand over his hair, then rubbed the back of his neck, a gesture Claire guessed he did whenever he felt uncomfortable. "I suppose... if you didn't mind running a Hoover around the sitting room..."

"A Hoover?"

"A vacuum cleaner."

"Oh. Right. Sure." He dug the vacuum, or Hoover, from a cupboard under the stairs. It looked ancient and judging from the patina of dust covering the machine, Claire doubted it saw much, if any, use.

"I'm just going to blitz the bathrooms," he said with a sheepish grin and Claire winced, because if the state of the kitchen was anything to go by, she did not want to see what the bathrooms looked like. Noah gave a little laugh, the sound wry. "They're not that bad, actually."

"Good to know."

Okay, enough. This was getting too weird. *And feeling too normal.* She'd vacuum the sitting room and then she'd go. They'd be even, having done favors for each other. The end.

The sitting room was through a low doorway that even Claire had to stoop under, and looked as lived in as the kitchen. Two sagging sofas framed a large fireplace with a huge wooden beam for a mantelpiece. There were several bookcases stuffed full of tattered Agatha Christies and Barbara Cartlands, and another bookcase held the more expected farming manuals and ordinance maps.

Quickly, she ran the Hoover around the room, chasing the giant dust bunnies that had collected under the sofas and chairs. She was just wrapping the cord around the handle of the machine when she caught sight of a photo, tinted in the sepia-like colors of a generation ago, of a woman with two boys standing in front of her. She had a hand on each of their shoulders, and a scarf covered her hair, hair the same color as Noah's. Even though the boys could have been no more than nine or ten, she recognized Noah as the younger one, dark-eyed and serious, with a shy, impish smile.

She stared at the photo for a long moment, transfixed by

the expressions on all of their faces: the mother's carefree smile and strangely sad eyes, the older boy looked proud and yet also defiant, and Noah, with his dark, quiet looks. She could almost feel the joy and pride radiating from his boyish self, as if he knew there was nothing better than standing next to his mother.

She heard Noah's steps on the stairs and she jumped away from the photo as if she'd been scalded, fumbling with the vacuum before she shoved it back inside the cupboard under the stairs amidst the jumble of boots and buckets and folding chairs. Dusting her hands on the back of her jeans, she turned to him with a bright smile.

"I've done the vacuuming, sorry, Hoovering. I think I'll just head back now."

"Of course, you've been brilliant, thank you." He hesitated, and then said, "I can run you back in the car but I don't want to miss—"

"Your daughter, of course." She hesitated too, because she wasn't sure what was worse: offering to walk, or waiting and meeting his daughter. "I can walk," she said, her voice coming out more firmly than she felt. She didn't want to play pretend happy families for even one second, and she didn't want to endure the girl's suspicion or hostility either. But it was also very dark outside.

"It's only ten minutes across the fields," Noah said. "I can give you a torch and some proper boots."

As opposed to her Prada ones. "Am I correct in assuming

a torch is a flashlight and not an open flame?" she said and Noah let out a rumble of a laugh.

"Yes, you are correct. We're not quite that behind the times out here in the sticks."

"Actually, I think I knew a torch was a flashlight," Claire admitted. "I always loved to hear my godmother say all the British words for things."

He arched an eyebrow at that. "Is Ruth your godmother?"

"Yes, but we hardly ever see each other. She and my mother were roommates at Vassar." And had grown steadily apart ever since.

"Let me get you some boots."

Five minutes later, she was standing outside the farmhouse, a pair of overlarge, mud-spattered Wellington boots on her feet and a huge flashlight, whose beam cut a swathe of light through the darkness, in her hand. It was a clear night, and the snow-covered fields were pristine, not even a single footprint marring their smooth whiteness.

"You just head straight that way," Noah said, pointing towards the field to the left of the house. He was standing close enough to her that she could smell him, soap and leather and a bit of sheep. "Walk to the end, down a bit of a slope, go over the stile, and you'll end up in Holly Cottage's garden."

"Okay." And hopefully she wouldn't end up wandering in the dark for hours, cold and lost.

"You're sure? I could run you—"

"No, it's fine." She pointed to the car headlights she saw at the end of the lane. "I think she's here." Noah turned, and before they could stumble through some awkward goodbyes, Claire set off for the field, the snow crunching under her boots.

In the distance she heard the slam of a car door, the muted sound of voices. Just a minute or two later the car drove off again, fast, as if the driver couldn't wait to get away.

Knowing she shouldn't, Claire turned anyway. Squinting, she could just make out Noah and a smaller, huddled figure clutching what looked like a pillow to her chest. Claire's heart twisted.

Shouldn't have looked. Shouldn't wonder, shouldn't care.

She turned back to the dark field stretching in front of her, the beam of her flashlight seeming weaker and less comforting than it had before, barely piercing the darkness. Resolutely, she walked on.

CHAPTER FIVE

NOAH WALKED INTO the house with Molly trailing behind him, clutching her pillow. In his mind's eye he could still see Claire setting off across the darkened fields, a slight figure against the night sky. He felt a twist of guilt at having her leave like that, but what choice had he had? He couldn't risk Dani pitching a fit about something, not when his custody arrangement was tenuous already.

Although in truth Dani hadn't even stayed to see her daughter inside; she'd been too intent on her own plans to bother about any of Noah's.

"So." He closed the front door and watched as Molly gazed around the kitchen with a kind of morose suspicion. She'd never been to his house before, and even though it was a good deal cleaner than it had been an hour ago, it wasn't anything like the townhouse Dani's parents had bought for her and their grandchild in York. He was conscious of the kitchen's low-ceilinged shabbiness; the smoke stains on the ceiling, the peeling paint on the woodwork, the scarred and warped oak table. Definitely not a chic townhouse in York's best neighborhood.

"Are you hungry?" he asked, and mutely Molly shook her head. Noah searched for something else to say. *This is going well.* About as well as their Saturday afternoons had gone, at any rate; he usually kept them busy doing something, and then they only had to endure the excruciatingly awkward conversation during dinner. Now he had four days of it to look forward to, and the worst part was, this wasn't how he wanted to be with his daughter. This wasn't how he wanted his daughter to be with him.

"What would you like to do?" he asked, his voice sounding just a little too loud. "The TV doesn't work but I have Netflix on my computer..." Although the Internet connection was so damn slow they'd be waiting hours for something to stream. And maybe he shouldn't have suggested they watch something; maybe he should have started a real conversation. But how?

Molly shook her head, so her dark hair, the same color as his, flew out around her face. "I'll just read my book," she said.

"Let me show you your room," Noah said.

He walked through the sitting room, as cramped and low as the kitchen, to the steep, narrow stairs that led upstairs. Molly paused on the bottom step, casting a glance around the sitting room with its faded sofas and blackened fireplace before turning to Noah in accusation.

"You don't even have a Christmas tree."

"That's true," Noah acknowledged as he struggled to

find some way to explain his complete lack of Christmas spirit. He had nothing Christmassy in the house at all; December twenty-fifth was just another workday as far as he was concerned, and had been ever since his mother had died when he was little more than Molly's age. But it couldn't be a workday this year.

"We could cut one down," he suggested. Molly pursed her lips, unconvinced. "There's a grove of pine trees on the other side of the fields. They'd be about the right size." He cast a glance at the ceiling. "Eight feet tall, I'd say, at least. We don't want some puny tree." He saw the tiniest flicker of interest light her eyes, the same brown as his, and he felt a wild surge of hope, of need to show his daughter they could do this. They could have a good time together. "Have you ever cut down your own Christmas tree before?"

"No," she said, and frowned.

"It'll be fun," Noah said, but he sounded desperate even to his own ears. "It'll be loads of fun."

Molly didn't answer, just walked up the stairs, shouldering past him. "Where's my room?" she asked when she was at the top, staring down at him, her pillow still clutched to her chest.

Any fledgling hope he'd been trying his damnedest to nurture sank like a stone. "Right down here," he said, and headed down the hall.

CLAIRE WALKED THROUGH the fields, the frozen snow crunching under her boots, the flashlight cutting a pale swathe of light through the darkness. The farther away she walked from Noah's house the lonelier she felt; with nothing but the empty expanse of endless fields around her, she felt as if she were the last person on earth, or at least in England.

Finally, after what felt like hours, but was in reality only about fifteen minutes, she saw Holly Cottage, the kitchen light she'd left on beckoning her with its comforting glow. She hurried towards it, climbing awkwardly over the stile that bridged the drystone wall that separated Noah's property from Ruth Carrington's, and then into the welcome warmth of the cottage.

She kicked off her boots and shrugged out of her coat, trying not to feel how empty and silent the cottage was, with only her in it. This was what she wanted, she told herself firmly. What she needed. She microwaved one of the ready meals she'd bought and made a fire in the woodstove in the living room. She opened a bottle of wine and retrieved the final exams she needed to mark, brought everything in on a tray and curled up by the fire.

Yes. This was perfect. This was exactly what she'd envisioned, what she'd longed for, when she'd left New York. Cozy solitude.

With a soft sigh, Claire leaned her head back against the sofa, closed her eyes, and thought of Noah. She'd kept him out of her thoughts by sheer force of will during the walk back to Holly Cottage, but she couldn't resist now, didn't even want to.

What were he and his daughter doing? Watching TV? Playing cards? She envisioned some happy family scene and her heart ached, although why or for what she refused to examine.

Don't go there, Claire. Don't buy into that broken dream.

She pulled the first essay towards her and took a slug of wine.

Identify two events that affected the United States' territorial expansion in the nineteenth century, and explain why and how they did.

Ugh. She was so not in the mood.

Pushing the essay, as well as her untouched chicken tikka masala-for-one aside, Claire tucked her knees up to her chest and took another sip of wine. She gazed into the fire, her emotions like a kaleidoscope within her. Turn it one way and she felt happy, even excited. Turn it another way, and she felt lonely and lost, a million miles from any place she'd called home.

She'd enjoyed being with Noah, even though it made a pang of something close to terror ripple through her. She was curious about him, about the solitary life he seemed to lead, and she'd liked brightening it just a little bit, even if it was just by wiping down his kitchen counters.

And that's how it starts, Claire. Haven't you learned anything?

With Mark it had been, of all mundane things, an umbrella. He'd left the teacher-parent meeting in the pouring rain, and she'd lent him her umbrella. She still remembered the little lurch of feeling the sight of him walking away under her red and blue striped umbrella had given her, a sense of belonging that was ridiculous and didn't even make sense.

And yet she'd felt it, and one little kindness had turned into, inch by inch, an almost-relationship. An almost disastrous relationship.

But you didn't get that far.

And she wouldn't get that far with Noah. She'd come to England to relax and recover, not fall for a man yet again.

And with that resolution firm in her mind, Claire drained her wineglass and headed for bed.

She woke the next morning to hazy blue skies and morning sunlight making the fields, still covered in snow, glitter as if they'd been strewn with diamonds.

She stood at the kitchen sink, a mug of coffee cradled in her hands, and let the beauty of the fresh, new day fill her with promise. She could make a picnic, take a long walk, or explore the village. And most importantly, get her car. Now that it had stopped snowing she should be able to dig it out herself.

She finished her coffee and bundled up before stepping outside, the cold stinging her cheeks, the crystalline air so clean and clear it felt like taking a drink of water.

Digging her gloved hands into the pockets of her coat, she was about to head down the lane that led towards the main road when she caught a blur of movement out of the corner of her eye. She turned and saw a slight figure huddled on top of the drystone wall, knees drawn up to skinny chest, shoulders slumped.

Even though she hadn't had a good look at her last night, Claire knew instinctively this was Noah's daughter. She hesitated, torn between a desire to help the girl, who looked clearly miserable, and the voice screaming in her head to stay uninvolved.

And yet how could she? Did Noah even know where his daughter was? Holly Cottage was a good fifteen minutes from his farm, plodding through snow-covered fields.

Besides, Molly looked small, maybe only seven or eight years old. Claire *had* to help.

Squaring her shoulders, she started over. As she came closer she saw the girl had a notebook on her knees, and was busily sketching something, her head bent over the paper. Claire took a step closer.

"Hey, there."

Startled, the girl whirled around, her eyes narrowing suspiciously as she caught sight of Claire. She sniffed, wiping her face with her arm, the other hand clutching the notebook.

"Hey."

"Are you Noah Bradford's daughter, by any chance?" Claire asked, and the girl's eyes narrowed further.

"How did you know that?"

"Lucky guess. He told me you were coming, and I know he lives right across there." She pointed in the direction of Ayesgill Farm.

The girl just hunched her shoulders further, tucking her chin towards her chest. Claire tried for a smile. "What are you drawing?" she asked, and in response the girl slammed her notebook shut; Claire had only glimpsed a few starkly drawn lines.

"Nothing."

"Does your Dad know you're out here?"

A brief and telling hesitation, and then she said, defiantly, "He doesn't even care."

"I'll bet he does," Claire answered steadily. "What's your name?"

"Molly."

"Hi, Molly, I'm Claire. And I was going to walk over to your dad's farm to return his flashlight. Torch, that is." She hadn't been intending to do that, having made a resolution to avoid Noah Bradford for the duration of her stay, but she would now. "Why don't you come with me? It's awfully cold out here."

Molly looked torn between telling Claire to shove it and wanting to cling to her. Such a little girl with so many big feelings, Claire thought sadly. She knew how that felt, trying to grapple with all the frustration and loneliness and fear. She'd had all the trappings of the perfect family, the perfect childhood, and that was all they'd ever been. Trappings.

"Fine," Molly finally said rather ungraciously, and scrambled off the wall.

They started across the field, the snow soft and wet now, having started to melt under the pale winter sunshine. Neither of them spoke, but Claire knew sometimes she just had to let the silence be, rather than fill it with so many empty words.

Still, she was hard pressed not to blurt out a question, because she was wondering whether Noah knew his daughter was out roaming the fields, or if he was worried about her. She also wondered why Molly looked so defensive and tucked in on herself, and who or what was the cause of her wariness. Noah—or her mother? Or someone else entirely?

The farmhouse had appeared on the horizon when Claire finally broke.

"Does your dad know you're out here, Molly?"

Molly tucked her chin against her chest. "No, but he was busy anyway. He doesn't care about me."

"Why do you say that?"

One bony shoulder lifted in a shrug. "He didn't even want me to come stay."

"I don't think that's true," Claire protested and Molly shrugged again. Claire thought about the conversation she'd overheard in the supermarket. Noah hadn't seemed as if he was unwilling to take Molly, but he'd been definitely reluctant. Claire suspected, however, that was because of the short notice, not that he didn't want to spend time with his daughter.

Or was she making assumptions, because she wanted him to be that way? She'd done the same with Mark. She'd bought into the whole trying-to-be-a-good-dad shtick he'd had going, hook, line, and sinker. Even the memory of how willingly gullible she'd been, when any number of signs had been glaring at her all along, made her cringe in shame.

"He hasn't even decorated for Christmas," Molly said suddenly. "There isn't even a *tree*." She turned to Claire, her eyes suspiciously bright even as she glared. "He didn't want me to come for Christmas. I *know* he didn't."

Claire opened her mouth to say *He wasn't expecting you for Christmas* when she closed it again, realizing that might not be the most sensitive thing to say. She had no idea what kind of arrangement Noah had with his ex, or why his daughter had been dumped on his doorstep at the last minute.

Her silence, however, seemed only to confirm Molly's belief that her father didn't want her there, for she pursed her lips and looked away, the classic kid's silent I-told-you-so. Claire sighed inwardly, wishing she were better equipped for these kinds of conversations.

As soon as they stepped into the farmyard, Noah's dog set up a frenzy of barking. Seconds later Noah flung open the door; he was wearing a thermal shirt, this one in dark gray, and another pair of faded jeans. Plain clothes, but he looked good in them. Amazing, actually, and Claire tried not to let her gaze linger on his taut belly or powerful thighs. This was a very inconvenient time to indulge her attraction.

"Molly…" Noah took a step towards his daughter, looking as if he wanted to grab her in a hug, or maybe shake her until her teeth rattled. Probably both. "Where were you?"

"I just went for a walk."

"You could have told me—"

Molly just sniffed, her chin jutted out, and shouldered past Noah into the house.

Noah watched her walk past before turning to Claire with a smile that would have seemed wry if there hadn't been so much sadness in his eyes. "You found her?"

"She was sitting on the wall outside Holly Cottage."

"I went out to check on the animals, and when I came back in she was gone. I was just about to go looking for her with Jake." He glanced down at the collie that was thrusting his head between Noah's knees, tongue lolling out.

Claire smiled at the sight even as her heart twisted in sympathy. "Things going okay?" she asked and he shrugged, jamming his hands into the pockets of his jeans.

"Not really. She's taken it into her head that I don't want her here and nothing I do or say seems like it's going to prove her otherwise."

"That's tough."

"Yeah." Noah squinted, his gaze on the snow-shrouded fields. "We haven't had an easy relationship," he said after a moment. "From the beginning."

Claire knew she shouldn't ask, shouldn't want to know, but the words bubbled up anyway. "Were you together with her mother for long?"

Noah's face darkened and he pressed his lips together. "It's complicated."

She definitely shouldn't have asked. Claire took a step back. "Well, I should go get my car."

"Your car! I completely forgot about it." Noah shook his head. "With Molly coming, it slipped my mind—"

"It's not your responsibility, Noah—"

"I said I'd help—"

She shrugged. "I can manage."

"I'm sure you can, but it will take you an age, doing it by yourself. Anyway, Molly and I could use a distraction." He turned back into the house. "Molly! Fancy an adventure?"

Claire didn't hear the girl's reply but moments later Molly came slinking out, arms folded across her chest. "What kind of adventure?"

"Claire's car is stuck in a snow bank. How about we dig it out, and then go find our Christmas tree?"

Molly's glance slid from Noah to Claire, and Claire could tell she was wondering just what was between her and Noah. Did she see Claire as some kind of threat?

"I arrived from the States yesterday," she said to Molly lightly. "I'm only staying for a week, but I managed to put my car right in a snow bank on the very first day."

She felt Noah give her a look, although what it signified

she had no idea. Had she been too obvious, stating how temporary her situation was? Not just for Molly's sake, but for Noah's, and most importantly, for hers.

Nothing about this will last.

"I suppose so," Molly said, and went inside to get her coat.

Ten minutes later, Noah had driven them to the road where Claire's poor Civic was buried under a mini-mountain of snow.

"Time to dig, I think," he said, and the four of them, Jake included, started chucking snow off the car.

Claire was focused on simply uncovering her car, when somehow an armful of snow hit her back. She turned around, but both Molly and Noah were still digging. Maybe it was an accident, she decided, and turned around again.

Wham. Another armful of snow hit her in the back, and when she whirled around this time Noah was looking all too innocent and Molly's gaze was darting between Claire and her dad, her expression one of cautious excitement.

Claire put her hands on her hips. "Are you trying to start a fight?"

Noah raised his eyebrows. "What are you talking about?"

She almost laughed aloud at his oh-so-innocent face. "I think you know very well what I'm talking about."

Noah turned to Molly, his innocent, bewildered expression endearingly exaggerated. "Do you know what she's talking about, Molly?"

Molly's gaze darted once more between the two adults, and Claire's heart twisted to see the slight confusion on the girl's features, as if she wasn't used to this kind of teasing, but she thought she might like it.

"No," she finally said. "I don't know what she's talking about."

"Okay, then," Claire said. "I guess it was my mistake." She gave them both a lingering look, and saw something flare in Noah's eyes. Relief that she was playing along, for Molly's sake? Or something else, something deeper, that she was already feeling in herself?

Don't fall for him, Claire. It will go nowhere.

It's just a snowball fight.

She heard the two separate voices in her head, the battle of her conscience, and decided, for the moment anyway, to ignore both.

She turned back to the car and as fast as she could, scooped up some snow, packed it into a ball, and then whirled around, flinging it towards Noah just as she saw him tossing an armful towards her.

"Argh!" Snow hit her full in the face and she wiped it away, her cheeks stinging from the cold, her eyes streaming. Her snowball, she saw, had landed harmlessly on Noah's chest, dusting his coat with snow. "Now you're asking for it," she said, and reached for more snow.

After that, things got pretty silly. All three of them started flinging snow, and Claire could hear Noah's trash-talking her—you call that *throwing*?—and Molly's sudden squeals of laughter. Both warmed her heart, even as her body froze under Noah's onslaught of well-aimed missiles.

After about fifteen minutes, she finally begged for mercy, cowering behind her mostly-uncovered car while Noah stood above her, hands on his hips, and Molly jumped up and down, more animated than Claire had ever seen her.

Claire glanced up at them both through her fingers, her hands covering her face. "And I thought you'd come out here to help me," she said in a mock whimper.

"Your car is uncovered, isn't it?" Noah answered.

He reached down to help her up, and Claire couldn't suppress the sparks that shot up her arm as she slid her gloved hand in his. She didn't even want to.

He pulled her up easily and she let go of his hand with reluctance, yet also as quickly as she could.

This was all getting just a little too cozy, and yet she craved it, the closeness, the fun, even the excitement. When had she last laughed like this? Not since Mark, certainly.

"Mostly uncovered," she told him with a nod towards her car, and with a few broad sweeps of his arm Noah had the rest of the snow off of it. "You want me to reverse it out of the bank?" he asked and although feminist pride made Claire tempted to say she could do it, she'd rather he did.

"Yes, please."

Minutes later Noah had her car in the middle of the road, facing the right direction. No reason, then, not to go home and curl up by the fire, mark a few essays.

And that sounds like so much fun. But perhaps a needed return to normality.

"Well, thank you for rescuing my car," she said, "even if you did soak me in the process. I'll leave you to get your Christmas tree." With an awkward little wave for them both Claire started towards her car.

Molly's wobbly voice stopped her in her tracks. "But aren't you coming with us?"

Chapter Six

CLAIRE TURNED AROUND to see Molly looking woebegone, and Noah clearly alarmed as he glanced down at his daughter.

"Claire's busy, Molly—"

Molly's face had closed up, her mouth pinched. She nodded once, accepting this explanation without a single argument, and that was what made Claire change her mind. If Molly had whined or pitched a fit, she might have been able to dismiss it as schoolgirl theatrics. But the way the little girl so silently, staunchly accepted someone disappointing her made everything in Claire ache.

"Not that busy," she said, and saw hope dawn in both Noah and Molly's eyes. "Where are you going to get the tree?"

"Dad's going to cut it down himself," Molly said, her voice touched with pride, and Claire could have wept at the look of surprised gratitude on Noah's face. She hadn't heard Molly call him Dad before.

"I've never cut down a tree myself," Claire said. "Or seen someone do it. This is definitely something I can't miss."

Ten minutes later, she'd driven her car back to Holly Cottage, and then piled into Noah's Land Rover to head back to Ayesgill Farm, where they picked up an old, weathered toboggan and a coil of rope to get the tree back to the house.

"And now," Noah said, "time to find the perfect tree."

Molly skipped ahead of them as they walked in the opposite direction of Holly Cottage, across the fields towards a dark crescent of pine trees, little more than a smudge on the horizon.

"Thank you," Noah said in a low voice as they followed Molly, their boots sinking deep into the soft, melting snow. "You're helping smooth the way with Molly, and I really appreciate it."

"It's no bother," Claire answered. Far from it.

"And yet you said you wanted a quiet Christmas by yourself," Noah reminded her. "I'm aware that snowball fights and cutting down Christmas trees isn't exactly that."

"No," Claire said after a moment.

She turned her head to gaze out at the white, rolling fields, the sky above a pale, fragile blue. The air was so cold and crisp it hurt to take a breath. Or maybe something else was making her hurt—memory and desire, twined together.

"You can bow out at any time," Noah said. "Molly obviously loves having you here, but I know I need to figure this out on my own. Don't—don't feel obligated."

She turned back to him, trying to smile, to keep it light.

"Even though you rescued me more than once?"

Noah took her question seriously, his gaze resting on her. "Even so. I know it's hard to say no to a kid, but she's not your responsibility."

Ouch. Claire tried not to flinch. It was stupid to feel hurt, because, of course, Molly wasn't her responsibility. She'd met the girl that morning. And she barely knew Noah, had no idea what was complicated about his relationship with his ex or his daughter.

Yet already she knew she was starting to fall.

"I'm having fun," she finally told Noah, her voice deliberately, painfully light. "I'll let you know when I'm not."

"Okay," he said, and seemed relieved that she wasn't being guilted into going along with him.

If only he knew the truth, she thought with something between a sigh and a wince. If only he knew how much she really wanted to be here, to belong. Wasn't that what she'd always been looking for? A real home. A real family.

A real Christmas.

NOAH SNUCK A sideways glance at Claire and wondered what she was thinking. He hated the thought that she'd come along because she pitied him, because she'd already seen how awkward his relationship with Molly was. He wanted to believe that she really was having fun, but he was afraid to believe it, because *he* was having fun. He couldn't even remember when he'd last enjoyed himself like this. He'd started a snowball fight, for crying out loud. He'd done it for Molly's sake, wanting to see her smile and hear her laugh, and yet he'd enjoyed it for his own sake, too.

Enjoyed seeing Claire's cheeks fill with color, hear the surprising sound of her laugh, high and clear. He was attracted to her, and probably had been since they'd first met. She was beautiful, in the elegant, restrained way of rich women. Yet when she'd laughed her cool composure had broken like a shell and he'd seen something real and warm underneath, something that interested him far more than Claire's cool beauty.

Dani had had that too, he reminded himself. Dani had had the rich girl thing going, and yet she'd also been real and warm and fun.

At first.

But it was stupid to compare Claire and Dani, stupid even to worry about it, because nothing was going to happen between him and Claire. She was here for a week, as she'd been at pains to remind him back by her car. And he didn't have room in his life for a woman anyway. Keeping the farm afloat took up all his energy and effort.

Molly had almost reached the trees, and Noah quickened his pace, his sheathed saw slung over his shoulder. Claire matched him, and they exchanged wry smiles as Molly pointed at a pine tree that had to be at least twenty feet high.

"I don't think that's going to fit in the sitting room,

Moll," Noah said. "We'd have to cut it in half."

"What about this one?" She pointed at another, more reasonably-sized tree, and Noah gave it a thorough examination.

"A little scrawny, don't you think?"

It quickly became a game, as he'd hoped it would, with all of them thinking of more and more ridiculous reasons to reject a tree. Noah had his eye on a straight Scots pine, and when they'd considered and rejected at least a dozen trees, he pointed it out to Molly with the air of someone who had finally hit the jackpot.

He saw Molly's face light up as she clasped her hands to her chest and he wondered, disbelievingly, if it were really this easy.

Molly was only eight years old. Did he win her loyalty, her *love*, by kidding around with snowballs and cutting down Christmas trees? Could it be that simple?

He realized he had no idea what kind of Christmases Molly had had before this. He had no idea, really, what kind of mum Dani was. He knew she had plenty of financial resources, with a well-to-do life funded by her parents, but did she tuck Molly in at night? Did she bake cookies with her? It just about killed him that he didn't know the answers to these questions. It was even worse that there was nothing he could do about it.

But if this Christmas visit with Molly went well, maybe he could ask for their custody arrangement to be changed.

Just the thought made everything in Noah lurch with both alarm and hope. Thanks to the power of Dani's parents, it had taken him a year to be able to see Molly at all. The first time he'd laid eyes on her, she'd been almost three years old.

The injustice of the court's verdict felt like a hole burning through his chest, and, with effort, he shoved the emotion away. He didn't want to spoil this afternoon by revisiting the sins of his past.

"Shall we cut it down?" he asked.

Molly nodded eagerly. Noah cleared some of the snow in front of the pine, unsheathed his saw and then lay down flat on his back. He scooted under the tree, breathing in the clean, pine scent from the tree's needles, and then started to saw.

Cutting down a pine tree was slow going, especially when the wood was filled with knots. After about ten seconds Molly dropped down to her knees and peered at him through the branches.

"Careful, Molly," he said. "This thing is sharp."

"Are you almost finished?"

He let out a laugh. "I've barely started."

"Can I try?"

He considered this for a few seconds. He'd grown up Ayesgill Farm, and had been handling a hammer, saw, and even an axe well before Molly's age. But Molly hadn't handled anything like that, and the thought of her getting hurt, of Dani blaming him for it, made his blood run cold.

But this was his life, and he wanted to share it with Molly. He wanted to give her something Dani couldn't, because God knew he couldn't afford all the treats and toys Dani could shower her with.

He would give her an experience she would remember, love and laughter that would stay with her for a long time.

"Come here," he said, and patted the area of flattened snow next to him. Molly scooted under the tree, and for a second he just savored the feeling of having his daughter next to him, both of them breathing in the scent of the pine needles. It was enough to make his throat close up with emotion, his heart beat fast with joy.

"Okay," he said finally. "Hold the saw like this. Do regular, even cuts, back and forth." He placed her little hands on the saw and guided her for a few moments, until she'd got used to its motion. He let go, watching her carefully, her lower lip jutted out, her eyes screwed up in concentration.

"This is *hard*," she panted, but didn't stop.

After a few minutes he had another turn, and then he scooted out from under the tree to look up at Claire. She'd been watching them, he saw, with a little smile on her face, softening her features.

"Your turn," he said, and Claire blinked in surprise.

"Me—"

"You didn't just come along for the ride, did you?" He held out the saw. "You said you'd never cut down a tree before. Now's your chance."

"Okay," Claire said after a moment, and she clambered under the tree too, so all three of them were squeezed together, sheltered by the branches.

"This *is* hard," Claire exclaimed when she had her turn with her saw.

Her hair brushed Noah's cheek as she moved and every time she pulled her arm back, her coat was pulled taut across her breasts and Noah couldn't keep himself from looking, or from a shaft of desire piercing him so sweetly.

He took over again, and then as they got closer to finally felling the tree, he had them do one cut each, taking turns with the saw, guessing who would make the final cut.

He made sure it was Molly, and he saw Claire give him a small, secretive smile, so he knew she understood. The tree was practically hanging by a thread when Molly finally made the last cut, and Noah pulled both Claire and Molly back as he nudged the tree with his boot to make sure it fell away from them.

"Timber," he announced cheerfully. "Now we've got to get this beauty home."

They all helped to load the tree on the toboggan, and then Noah bound it with rope. He clowned around for Molly's sake, pretending the toboggan was too heavy to pull, before they started the trek back to Ayesgill Farm. As the farmhouse came in view, the most familiar sight in the world to him with its whitewashed stone walls and slate roof, a curl of bluish-gray smoke snaking up towards the sky from its chimney, he felt a powerful surge of feeling—whether it was love or joy or gratitude, he didn't know. It was good, of that he was sure. He felt, for the first time in a long while, that he was truly coming home.

IT WAS ALL so weirdly, wonderfully normal to come into Noah's house as he unbound the tree. Claire took off her coat and boots, and hung up her and Molly's gloves and scarves on the rail of the Aga, savoring the warmth that rolled out from the battered beast of a stove for a moment.

"Can we have hot chocolate?" Molly asked hopefully, and Claire thought she remembered seeing some cocoa in Noah's overflowing shopping cart yesterday.

"I don't see why not," she said, and bustled about the kitchen in search of a pan and milk, sugar, and cocoa. Was it wrong to enjoy these little domestic tasks so much, she wondered, or just stupid? Dangerous, maybe. It wasn't as if this were real. But it was so fun, so lovely to pretend, for just a little while, that this was her life. Her home.

Husband, child. A family. A cozy kitchen, the dog sprawled out on the floor in front of the Aga, so she had to step around him as she made the hot chocolate. Jake seemed used to it.

Molly sat on one of the stools by the kitchen island, a huge rectangle of chopping block that yesterday had been covered with junk mail and dirty dishes, but was now still swept clean.

Outside the sun sparkled on the snow and in the distance she heard Noah wrestling the Christmas tree into the sitting room. All of it together, the sounds, the sights, the smells, made Claire feel as if she'd stepped into a daydream. *A fantasy.*

And for a few minutes, maybe an hour, she could enjoy it. Surely that wouldn't hurt anyone?

The hot chocolate was simmering on top of the Aga and Claire had just located some mugs, giving them a discreet rinse before placing them on the counter in front of Molly, when Noah came in, stamping snow from his boots, his cheeks red from the cold.

"I got the tree inside. Now I just need to figure out how to put it up."

"Don't you have a tree stand?" Claire asked, and Molly piped up,

"What about decorations? Ornaments and icicles and a star for the top?"

"I'm not sure I have any of that," Noah said with a rueful smile, and Molly looked at him in incredulous pity.

"Haven't you had a Christmas tree before?"

"Not for a long time," Noah said, and there was a sadness to his voice that made Claire wonder why he hadn't. Where was his family—the sibling she'd seen in that photograph, his parents?

"Well, what about when you were little?" Molly pressed.

"Didn't you have a Christmas tree then?"

Noah got a strange look on his face, almost as if he'd been sucker-punched. He didn't say anything for a moment, and Claire, sensing that some memory or feeling had been prodded, hurried to fill the silence.

"How about some hot chocolate?" She passed a bag of mini-marshmallows, yet another item Noah had thrown into his shopping cart yesterday, to Molly. "Why don't you put a few marshmallows in each cup?"

She poured the hot chocolate and Molly diligently counted out the marshmallows, making sure each mug had the same amount. Claire glanced at Noah out of the corner of her eye, and saw that he was staring into space, in the grip of some memory. She couldn't tell from his face whether it was a good or bad one.

"Noah?" she prompted, holding a mug out to him, but he just shook his head as if rousing himself from a dream and with a muttered apology left the room.

CHAPTER SEVEN

WHILE MOLLY DRANK her hot chocolate, Claire tidied the kitchen and then investigated the contents of the ancient fridge, hoping she'd find something to give the girl for lunch.

There were the makings for sandwiches, and she'd just put it all out on the counter and opened a can of tomato soup, when Noah reappeared in the kitchen, a battered cardboard box in his arms.

"Here we are," he said, and his voice came out sounding strange, a little croaky.

Molly looked up from her hot chocolate, a cocoa mustache coating her top lip.

"Decorations," Noah explained, and then cleared his throat. "Ornaments." He put the box on the counter and then took a step back, almost as if it were a ticking bomb that might go off at any second.

Oblivious of her father's discomfort, Molly abandoned her hot chocolate and reached for the lid of the box. "Where did you get these?" she asked and Noah gave a little shrug.

"In the storage loft. They haven't been used in a long

time."

"Be careful, Molly," Claire said quickly, for she could see that some of the ornaments looked fragile. All of them looked old and well-loved, once upon a time, and they made her wonder about the boy who had once hung them on the tree... and the man who, it seemed, never had.

"Look at this!" Molly exclaimed, and lifted up a pinecone dusted with silver glitter, a red yarn ribbon tied around one end. "Did you make this?"

Noah's mouth quirked in a tiny half-smile. "I think that was me. I was generous with the glitter. David was much more careful."

"David?" Claire asked before she could help herself.

"My brother."

"And what about this one?" Molly held up a hand-knit Santa, complete with white yarn beard and a red hat with a white pompom.

"My mum knit that," Noah said. "Your grandmother."

Molly's eyes brightened with curiosity as she turned to Noah, the Santa still held aloft in her hand. "Where is she?"

"She died a long time ago, Molly." Noah gave her an apologetic smile. "I was only about your age."

"And what about your father?" Molly asked slowly. "My grandfather." Claire could see the girl was making connections, pieces clicking into place as her father became more of a real person, someone with family himself, with a history.

"He died too, five years ago," Noah said quietly.

"Did I ever meet him?"

Pain flashed across his face like lightning and he shook his head. "No."

Molly looked as if she wanted to ask more questions, and some deep-rooted instinct made Claire swoop in.

"These ornaments look great. How about we finish our hot chocolate and then hang them on the tree?"

Molly picked up her cup, thankfully distracted, and Noah's gaze met Claire's over the top of the little girl's head, his mouth curving in a smile of gratitude.

And even though it wasn't anything much, just a smile, Claire felt a shivery rush of sensation through her insides. Noah Bradford's smile *did* things to her.

They finished their hot chocolate and ate the sandwiches and soup Claire had made, and then Noah hefted the box into the sitting room where he'd managed to rig the tree up, next to the fireplace. Soon Molly was busy retrieving the treasured ornaments from the box, exclaiming over each one before hanging them on the tree.

Noah sat on the sofa and watched her, a smile on his face that made Claire ache to see it. He looked so happy and sad at the same time, both proud and regretful. Sharing Christmas with the daughter he never saw had to be bringing all sorts of emotions to the forefront.

"Aren't you going to hang any?" Molly asked Claire after she'd put at least a dozen on the tree.

"Oh, I don't know..." Somehow, even though she'd

been spending time with them all day, hanging ornaments on the tree felt like an intrusion into their family.

"Go on," Noah encouraged her. "You aren't that much of a Scrooge, are you?"

"A Scrooge," she exclaimed in only semi-mock outrage. "I'm not a Scrooge."

Noah arched an eyebrow, his gaze locked on hers. "Yet you wanted to spend Christmas by yourself?"

"As did you," she shot back, and then could have bitten her tongue. What would Molly think if she believed her father wanted to spend Christmas on his own? Thankfully she hadn't seemed to have heard; she was hanging a large glass globe filled with fluttering golden stars on the tree.

"I didn't think I had any choice," Noah said and Claire cocked her head.

"Isn't there anyone you could have spent Christmas with?" she asked quietly, so Molly wouldn't hear.

Noah shrugged. "My brother David, maybe. But he's busy with his own life and family."

She frowned. "Aren't you part of that family?"

"I'm a bit of a black sheep." Noah leaned forward and took an ornament from the box; it was a silver snowflake, just a little bit tarnished. "Here you go."

Silently, Claire took it from him, her fingers brushing his as his gaze held hers. A black sheep, who stayed to run his family farm?

Why wasn't he close to his brother? What had his childhood been like, if his mother had died when he was no more than Molly's age? She wanted to know the answers to those questions and more, Claire thought as she turned and hung the snowflake on the tree. She wanted to know more about this man.

She didn't get a chance to ask Noah any questions, though, for Molly bounced back towards them with more ornaments, insisting that Noah take his turn, and then all three of them were decorating the tree until the box was empty and the boughs were weighed down with balls and baubles, knitted Christmas figures and painted pine cones.

As soon as the tree was done Molly planted her hands on her hips and looked around at the rest of the sitting room with its shabby sofas and worn rugs, the bookcases stuffed with old paperbacks, and the fireplace taking up nearly a whole wall.

"Nothing else is decorated," she stated, and then looked at both Noah and Claire expectantly. "Do you have any more decorations up there?"

"I'm not sure..." Noah answered slowly. "I could look, I suppose."

"How about we go outside to cut some holly and evergreen for the mantelpiece while your dad looks?" Claire suggested. "It will smell so nice in here."

Noah gave her another grateful look before disappearing upstairs, and Claire and Molly got on their coats and boots before whistling for Jake and heading outside.

There were some holly trees right outside the farmhouse, and a few evergreens not too far away. In very little time they had armfuls of fragrant greens that they brought back into the house.

Claire cleared the mantel of stacks of old bills and newspapers, putting the papers in the recycling bin on the porch and the bills in the stack she'd already made in the kitchen. She was, she knew, becoming rather familiar with Noah's house and its once-messy contents.

Molly helped her arrange the evergreen and holly, and Claire found some candles in a drawer in the Welsh dresser in the kitchen. When they'd put the candles among the greens, they both stepped back, satisfied with their handiwork.

"That looks fantastic," Noah said as he came down the stairs with another box. "I forgot my mum used to do the same." He sounded surprised and just a little sad, and Claire's heart twisted again at the thought of his loss.

"What do you have there?" Molly asked and Noah opened the box.

"A Nativity set," he said. "I used to love playing with it when I was little." He took out all the pieces: shepherds and kings, Mary and Joseph, a sleepy-looking angel and the manger with baby Jesus. "And don't forget these," he said with a smile, and took out two sheep.

"Can I set it all up?" Molly asked eagerly and with a nod Noah cleared the deep windowsill that looked out over the farmyard. "How about here?"

Molly began arranging the pieces and as she watched her Claire realized with a jolt that it was already getting dark outside. Granted, in Yorkshire that meant it was only four o'clock, but still. She'd spent nearly the entire day with Noah and his daughter.

And what a lovely day it's been.

"I should go," she said quietly as they both continued to watch Molly. "It's late, and you'll want time with Molly…"

"Don't," Noah said quickly, the word, and the urgent tone he'd spoken it with, seeming to surprise them both. "She likes having you here," he added in a more measured voice. "And I do, too. Why don't you stay for dinner?"

Claire couldn't ignore the sense of happiness ballooning inside her, making her feel as light as air. She pursed her lips with a teasing look. "I think you just want me to cook for you."

"That too," Noah answered with a grin. "I'm not so bad with the basics, but…"

"I don't mind." She wanted to cook for them, Claire realized. She wasn't much of a cook, but she longed to try. And yet hadn't she been here before, worming her way into someone's family because she wanted to belong? But Noah was so different from Mark.

He wasn't, after all, Claire acknowledged with a sour churning of guilt and memory, married.

Noah watched Molly set up the Nativity set a dozen different ways as Claire went into the kitchen to make dinner. He followed her with his gaze, noticing the subtle sway of her hips, the way her skinny jeans clung to her slender curves, her long hair falling down her back in a dark waterfall. The little pulses of attraction he'd felt all day turned into an overwhelming surge of longing.

This can't go anywhere. You know that.

But he wasn't ready to let the day end. It had been just about the best day he'd had in… well, since he could remember.

Molly had started playing with the Nativity set pieces as if they were dolls, and so Noah got up and went to start a fire. He sat back on his heels, enjoying the crackling blaze, its cheering warmth, and the sounds he could hear around him—Molly playing quietly to herself, the clank of pots and pans from the kitchen as Claire hummed a few bars of *Walking in a Winter Wonderland.*

Noah smiled, his heart as full as it had ever been. For the last five years he'd lived like a monk, or a hermit, tending the farm, trying to make ends meet, his social life consisting of no more than a nod to a person in passing or the few, fumbled hook-ups he'd had with women in York or Newcastle, when he'd gone there for business. Not much of a life of all.

And this isn't either.

But he decided to ignore the annoying little voice and

just run with the enjoyment and pleasure the day was giving him. It was only one day, after all.

A little while later, Claire called them into dinner, and Noah nearly did a double take at the sight of the kitchen table, yesterday covered with papers and dirty dishes, now laid for three, complete with napkins.

"It's just a chicken stew," Claire said, making a face. "Nothing fancy."

"I don't like fancy," Noah assured her. He usually subsisted on beans and toast, with the occasional fried egg or bowl of plain pasta thrown in for variety's sake.

"It looks delicious," Molly piped up and Claire smiled and sat down, tucking her hair behind her ears.

They ate in companionable silence for a few moments, and then Molly asked what they were doing tomorrow. Noah knew the 'they' meant the three of them, and he wondered uneasily what Claire thought about that. He and Molly were hijacking her holiday plans. She'd said she wanted to be alone, and here she was, playing happy families, cooking dinner, and hanging ornaments.

Maybe she was just taking pity on him. The prospect made everything in him cringe. He'd had enough pity, as well as a fair amount of scorn, for the choices he'd made in life. He wasn't about to take anymore.

"Noah?" Claire's voice, soft and questioning, broke into the storm of his thoughts. He looked up, blinking.

"Sorry?"

"It's just," Claire said with a small smile, "you suddenly started frowning pretty ferociously. Molly and I wondered what you were thinking about."

"Just thinking about checking on the animals," Noah said quickly. He smiled at Molly, and she looked back at him uncertainly. She had a wary look in her eyes again, the way she had when she'd first come here. He'd thought that self-protective suspicion had gone, what with the snowball fight and the Christmas tree, but it was still there. Of course it was still there. Nothing changed overnight. Nothing good, anyway.

"Sorry," he said again, and Molly asked once more what they were doing tomorrow. "Let's leave it for now," Noah advised, trying to keep his voice light and easy. "See what the weather's like."

"It's Christmas *Eve* tomorrow," Molly said in an aggrieved, quavering voice. "Aren't we going to do something special?"

It was Christmas Eve *tomorrow?* Noah hadn't even realized that, to his own shame. "What would you like to do?" he asked and then forced himself to ask another question. "Do you usually do something special with your mum?"

Molly glanced away. "Not really," she mumbled, and Noah wished he knew more about Dani's parenting. Not that he'd ever had a choice or say in the matter, but... it would have been good to know.

"There's a children's service tomorrow, at the church in

the village," Claire said. "I saw it when we drove past, going to the supermarket."

Noah turned to Molly. "Do you want to go, Moll?"

He watched as his daughter swung her wide-eyed gaze towards Claire. "Are you going?"

Claire's glance skittered between Noah and Molly, and his insides clenched. Talk about being put on the spot.

"Well…" she began uncertainly, and Noah jumped into the breach.

"Claire most likely has her own plans, Molly. But we can go, just the two of us."

He almost thought he saw hurt flash across Claire's features before her expression smoothed out. "I'll clear the plates," she said, and rose from the table.

Molly's face had closed and she hunched forward, reminding him of how she'd looked yesterday, how awkward things had been between them, and how fragile they were now. Had he really thought it was that easy, that he'd toss a snowball and cut down a tree and his relationship with his daughter would be magically fixed?

It wasn't him, he realized, that had softened Molly and made her smile. It was Claire. It was the whole package—a proper family, a real Christmas.

Things, it seemed, that Dani hadn't given her.

"I'm going to go draw," Molly mumbled, and slid off her chair, disappearing silently into the sitting room. Noah sat back in his chair with a weary sigh.

"Coffee?" Claire asked, a note of uncertainty in her voice. "Or I could just go, if you two want to be alone…"

"I think," Noah said, trying for wryness, "that we definitely do not want to be alone. And I'll make the coffee. You've done enough." He rose from the table while Claire sat down, the smile she gave him uncertain but, he hoped, genuine.

He really didn't want her to go, and not just because of how Molly had taken to her. *He'd* taken to her. Stupid and irrational as that was. He could list the reasons why starting anything with Claire Lindell was a mistake. She was clearly rich, privileged, and wouldn't be interested in anything to do with a Yorkshire sheep farmer except, perhaps, the proverbial roll in the hay.

And what's so wrong with that?

He fumbled with the cups he'd been retrieving from the cupboard, nearly dropping one on the floor. In the last five years on the farm, he'd had nothing remotely approaching an actual relationship, not since Dani. He wasn't willing to risk being burned again, and especially not with someone who was like Dani in so many ways.

The only thing Claire has in common with Dani is that they're both rich.

And if he and Claire both agreed to a fling, a one week type of thing… what, really, was the harm in that?

Not, he acknowledged, that Claire had given off any signals of wanting such a thing. Hell, he wasn't even sure if he wanted it. Been there, done that when it came to meaning-less sex. He didn't know if he was ready to risk a relationship with anyone, but another one-night stand or temporary fling?

As attracted as he was to Claire, the prospect didn't really appeal. What appealed was more of what they'd already been experiencing: family-like dinners, cutting down Christmas trees, laughing and talking together.

God help him.

"Penny for your thoughts." Claire's light voice interrupt-ed the hurtling trajectory of his thoughts, much to his relief.

"Nothing much—"

"You're scowling again." She rose from the table and went to take the whistling kettle off the Aga. He hadn't even noticed it had come to the boil. "Do you need to check on the animals? I can stay here with Molly while you do."

"That would be great," Noah said. He needed to clear his head, get a little space. A little perspective. "I won't be long," he promised, and with the coffee forgotten he practically bolted from the kitchen.

Chapter Eight

A BIT BEMUSED by the non-conversation she'd just had with Noah, Claire tidied the kitchen, loading the dishwasher and wiping the counters. She had no idea what was going on in Noah's head, why he'd suddenly started looking kind of ferocious, but she didn't really think it had anything to do with the animals.

If he didn't want her here, Claire decided, he had to let her know. She'd ask him outright. She wasn't about to make the same mistake of insinuating herself into people's lives again.

With that resolved, she went to find Molly. She found the girl curled up in the window seat, her knees tucked up to her chest, the Nativity set scattered around her, the pieces she'd arranged with such happy care now tumbled over, lying on their sides. Claire's heart lurched at the sad sight.

"Molly?" She sat down next to her, righting the figure of Joseph. Molly nudged it over again with her foot.

Neither of them spoke for a moment; Claire was trying to figure out what to say. Something had gone wrong since dinner, which shouldn't really surprise her. Clearly Molly's living arrangement was a difficult one, and one happy day wasn't going to make everything better.

Molly finally broke the silence. "I want to go home."

Claire's heart lurched again. "It's natural to feel a little homesick when you're in a strange place," she said after a tiny pause. "Especially at night. Would you like me to read you a story?"

Molly gave her a look of such disdain that Claire couldn't help but recoil a little bit. "I'm not a baby."

"Of course you're not," Claire agreed. "Sorry. Stupid idea."

"Why aren't you coming to church with us tomorrow?" Molly asked, her lower lip trembling even as her eyes glared defiance.

"I..." Claire gazed at her helplessly. "I think your dad might enjoy some alone time, just the two of you."

"Yeah, *right*." Molly shook her head, her voice dripping scornful disbelief. "He's never wanted that before."

"Molly, I don't know everything that's happened between you and your dad," Claire began carefully. "But I'm pretty sure he loves you a lot, and he's thrilled to have you here for Christmas." Molly just shook her head and looked away. "That doesn't mean things won't be weird or uncomfortable sometimes," Claire continued doggedly. "But you just need to work through it."

"You sound like such a *grownup*," Molly said scathingly, and with one last shove for the poor Nativity set, the pieces tumbling onto the floor, she got up from the window seat and ran upstairs.

Claire sat, the room dark, save for the light from the fire which had burned down to embers, and wondered what she should do. Part of her was insisting this wasn't her problem and she shouldn't get involved, because she was, realistically, nothing to these people. She'd met them yesterday, for heaven's sake.

And yet she still cared. More than she should, but she couldn't deny her own feelings. But maybe, she acknowledged with a sigh, she should shut them down. It wasn't as if any of this was going anywhere.

She heard the back door open and the already-familiar stamp of Noah's boots as he came into the kitchen and shook the snow off. A few seconds later he appeared in the doorway of the sitting room, stopping in silence as he took in Claire's rather dejected form on the window seat, the scattered Nativity pieces.

He moved to the fireplace and tossed a few logs onto the fire, stoking up the embers into a comforting blaze. "Let me get that coffee," he murmured, and disappeared again.

Claire listened to him moving around the kitchen, the sounds so comforting, and leaned back against the window and closed her eyes. She felt tired and weirdly homesick; although what she missed she couldn't say. Something, she feared, she'd never really had.

A few moments later she heard Noah's footsteps and

then felt his hand touch her shoulder. She opened her eyes, and that homesickness feeling crashed over her in a wave, for the look on his face was one of tender concern, and it made her *want* things. So many things.

"Thanks," she murmured, and took the mug of coffee from, cradling it in her hands and letting its warmth seep into her.

"I'm sorry about Molly," he said as he sat opposite her on the window seat.

"There's nothing to be sorry for. She's clearly going through a tough time."

"I'll go up and check on her in a minute," Noah said, "but I think she might need a little alone time. And I think you deserve an explanation."

"An explanation?"

"Of why things are the way they are between us. Me and Molly," Noah clarified hastily, the faintest blush touching his cheeks. Claire took a sip of coffee and wondered just how things were between them. Her and Noah.

"I went out with Molly's mother Dani for a few years, when I was just a kid really," Noah began in a low voice. "We weren't a good match. I was a farmer's kid, definitely rough around the edges, and she was from a rich family in York. Big house, private school, all of it. We met at a pub and I suppose it was love, or really, lust at first sight. She was fun and bubbly, and I wanted a good time. An escape from home, too."

"Why did you need an escape from home?" Claire asked quietly.

"I told you and Molly my mother died when I was nine." He gave a little shrug. "Home wasn't that great. My father buried himself in running the farm, which was understandable because it was going under. My brother David was just trying to get out of Ledstow as fast as he could."

"And you?" Claire asked. Noah gave her a bleak smile.

"I was trying to hold it all together, I suppose. Cooking meals, keeping the place clean, helping my father. But I was just a kid, and I didn't manage very well. When I was eighteen I got accepted to Bishop Burton Agricultural College and had just finished my first year when I met Dani." He was silent for a moment, seeming lost in his memories, and Claire just waited for him to gather his thoughts. "She was out of control from the beginning, but I didn't see it." Another silence, and Claire watched his eyes shadow and his mouth firm. He gave a slight shake of his head as he continued, "I just loved how fun she was. Everything was a game to her, an adventure. And I liked how she took me away from everything going on at home. But after a few months I started to see how she was on self-destruct mode. Drinking too much, probably using drugs, although she never did around me. Her moods, swinging from high to low and back again." Another pause, and he let out a weary, defeated sigh. "Stealing from her parents."

"And something happened," Claire prompted gently

when Noah didn't seem inclined to say anything more. He nodded heavily.

"Yes, something happened. She stole a bunch of jewelry from her mother. Really expensive stuff, I don't even know what. Family heirlooms." He shook his head again. "I don't even know why she did it. Her parents gave her a generous allowance, and paid for her flat while she was at university. But maybe it was never about the money. Maybe she just wanted attention. As far as I could tell, they were completely self-obsessed with themselves and their social standing."

It was, Claire acknowledged with a hollow feeling, an all-too familiar story. Thankfully she'd never gone off the rails the way Dani seemed to have done.

But you almost did. You came very, very close.

"So what happened when she stole all the jewelry?" Claire asked.

"She blamed me." He looked up with a bleak smile. "And of course her parents believed her. They'd never liked me, assumed I was a bad influence. And maybe I was." He was silent for a moment, considering. "I never called her on any of her crap. Maybe I should have."

"You can't blame yourself—"

He shrugged. "I chose to get involved with her, to stay involved with her even after I knew she was spiraling out of control." He paused, took a deep breath and let it out slowly. "And I choose to take the blame when she pointed the finger at me."

Claire's mouth dropped open. "What—"

"I had no proof that I didn't steal the stuff, and her parents would never believe me over her," Noah explained with a shrug. "Besides, I knew she adored her parents even if they never seemed to have time for her, just money. I didn't want to shatter whatever they did feel for her." He paused and then added quietly, "And I loved her, even though I knew it was crazy."

Tears stung Claire's eyes and she blinked them back rapidly. "I know what that's like."

"Do you?" He gave her a lingering look, seeming to want to say more. "Anyway, it landed me in prison for eighteen months. Her parents knew the judge, and I got the maximum sentence. So I never finished college or any of that. And when I'd been inside for just a couple of weeks, Dani wrote and told me she was pregnant."

"Oh, Noah," Claire said softly.

"I read her the riot act, as much as I could from prison." He smiled wryly. "I told her she had to clean up her act, take care of herself." He scrubbed his face with his hands. "It was terrible, knowing I was so powerless to help her or do anything. And then when I got out her parents stacked it so I had no involvement with Molly. They claimed I was a *risk* to her." His voice choked on the word and he looked away.

"The irony was," he continued after a moment, his voice low and level again, "they weren't even interested in her. Dani told me they never saw her. They just set Dani and

Molly up in a townhouse in York and threw money at them. I didn't get to see Molly until she was nearly three. And since then it's only been Saturday afternoons, in York. I've been afraid to ask for more, in case her parents come down hard again. They have the power. But maybe I should." His face settled into grim lines. "Maybe I should," he said again, quietly, and Claire longed to touch him, a squeeze of his hand or a touch of his shoulder. She didn't move, but she ached with the need to comfort him.

"I should go check on Molly," he said after a moment, and drained his coffee cup. "But don't go yet. I still want to talk to you."

A wary thrill ran through her at his words and she nodded from behind her coffee cup. "Okay."

Noah went upstairs and Claire took their empty mugs into the kitchen, rinsing them in the sink and tidying up a bit more, wanting to keep busy. She had no idea what Noah wanted to talk to her about when he came back downstairs. Was it stupid to feel a heady mix of hope and fear? Was she reading too much into such small, simple things?

He'd helped her with her car; she'd helped him with his kid. Maybe that's all it was. But he'd told her so much about himself, and her heart ached for him. She didn't want this just to be tit for tat.

"She's asleep."

Claire whirled around, one hand pressed to her chest. Noah stood in the doorway of the kitchen, his face cast in shadow so she couldn't read his expression. He took a step into the room, but even in the light she still couldn't tell what he was thinking—or feeling.

"She was shattered," he continued, and it took Claire a second to realize he meant tired. Her godmother said that sometimes. *Shattered.* It was how she felt, and not in a tired kind of way. "A big day."

"Yes."

"I wanted to tell you, though," he continued in his low, steady voice, "that I didn't mean to hijack your quiet holiday. Molly's taken a liking to you, and you've made things so much easier between us, so I want to thank you for that, but you don't need to feel like you have to be here—"

"*Don't,*" Claire interjected, her voice coming out shamefully choked. "Don't *thank* me."

Noah took a step towards her. "Claire—"

She turned away, hating that she was so near tears. So it had been tit for tat, after all. Simply doing each other favors. Stupid, stupid Claire.

"I've said something wrong," Noah said quietly. Claire took a deep breath and brushed at her eyes before turning around.

"No, you haven't. You're kind to let me off the hook, but I've wanted to be here. I wouldn't have agreed if I hadn't."

"I've wanted you to be here," Noah answered quietly.

"But you want time alone with Molly," Claire finished

for him. Noah shook his head, and then gave her a wry smile.

"I do, of course I do, because she's my daughter. But having you here has been good—for both of us. It's smoothed out the rough edges between Molly and me, and..." He paused, seeming to search for words. "I've really enjoyed it," he finished. "Everything. Snowball fights, cutting down the Christmas tree, even just sitting around drinking hot chocolate. I'm... glad you've been here." He smiled awkwardly, his cheeks touched by a faint flush, and Claire smiled back at him, her heart thudding hard.

"I've been glad, too," she told him.

"So you don't mind not having a quiet Christmas?" Noah asked with a crooked smile, and Claire shook her head.

"I'm not sure I ever wanted that in the first place. I was just running away."

"From what?"

How much to tell, to confess? "From my mistakes." He arched an eyebrow, waiting, and she continued hesitantly, "I was involved with a man. Not very involved, not... well." No need to get graphic. "But it ended badly. It would have ended very badly, if I'd kept going with it." She could see the confusion on Noah's face and knew she needed to spell it out. "He was married."

"Oh." There was no condemnation in Noah's voice, just understanding.

Even so, Claire felt tears threaten and she had to blink

rapidly, swallow hard. She hadn't told anyone this. Who could she have told? Her friends and faculty at Stirling would have been shocked, and rightly so. She might have lost her job. As for her family...

"So what happened?" Noah asked quietly.

Claire took a ragged breath. "His daughter Emma was— is—one of my students. Mark." She was silent for a moment, trying to order her thoughts, and Noah waited, his gaze steady, so steady on her. The look in his eyes gave her the courage to tell him the whole truth, the confidence to know he wouldn't judge her... even if she already had judged herself. "Emma is one of my best students. One of my favorites. I was helping her with a special research project she was doing for extra credit, and so we spent a lot of time together, just the two of us, after school. Mark would pick her up from those sessions, and so I got to know him that way."

The corner of his mouth quirked upwards even as the look in his eyes remained both sad and understanding. "And one thing led to another?"

"Basically." She let out a shaky laugh. "Emma invited me to an exhibit at the Natural History Museum. It related to her research topic, and I wanted to encourage her. Mark came with us, and it felt..." Like a family. How could she explain how lovely it had felt to be part of things, when the same thing was happening here and now, with Noah and Molly?

History was repeating itself, and maybe that was because she intended it to do so. She just couldn't help herself.

"Claire." Noah stepped forward and took her by the shoulders. Claire blinked at him, jolted from his thoughts, surprised by his closeness. "Stop beating yourself up over this," he told her. "There's no point. Trust me, I've been there, done that for way too long already."

"It's hard not to," she whispered.

"I know." He smiled sadly down at her.

A thrill ran through her as she became aware of his hands, so warm and solid on her shoulders, almost brushing the tops of her breasts. His face was close to hers, close enough she could see the way his lashes swept his cheeks when he blinked, and how his five o'clock shadow's worth of stubble glinted in the dim light. She breathed in the smell of him—leather and wood and a little sheep. A pleasant, masculine smell. A Noah smell.

How can you already know his smell?

But she did, and she craved it. Craved him.

Gently, he brushed a tendril of hair from her cheek, tucked it behind her ear. Claire's breath hitched and every sense and sinew strained and waited, wanting him to kiss her. Needing him to.

And he almost did. He lowered his head, and her lips parted in expectation. She very nearly stood on her tiptoes to close that little space between their mouths.

But then Noah eased back with the kind of apologetic,

self-deprecating smile that made Claire want to weep in an entirely different way.

"So what happened?" he asked, and it took Claire a minute to compose herself, to pretend she hadn't just been waiting with every sense and sinew for him to kiss her.

"I finally woke up," she said simply. "I realized what was happening. We'd been spending a lot of time together by then—both with Emma and just the two of us. He told me his wife worked all the time, didn't care about him or Emma." She held up a hand to forestall him, even though he hadn't looked as if he were about to say anything. "I know that's what they all say. And it's no excuse at all, anyway."

He gave her a faint smile. "I know you know that."

"How would you know what I know?" she asked with a shaky laugh.

"You're a good person, Claire."

More tears sprang to her eyes and she couldn't quite blink these ones away. One escaped, trickling down her cheek as she whispered her confession. "I don't feel like I'm a good person. I feel like I came a hair's breadth from selling my soul. From betraying everything I am and believed in, and for what? A little happiness? Not even a little. It was all lies, anyway. His wife did care about them. I realized that—after." She'd crept out of Mark's bedroom, ashamed and sick at heart at how close she'd come to having an affair with a married man, and had seen a note scribbled by Emma's mother to the two of them stuck in the hall mirror.

Such a small thing, and yet so vital. Those little, easy words spoke of a love and affection that Mark had pretended wasn't there. And when Emma had opened her bedroom door and seen, in appalled silence, her history teacher creeping out of her apartment after midnight, her clothing rumpled and her hair in a tangle about her face…

With a terrible, burning shame, Claire had realized just how much of an intruder and impostor she'd really been.

And was the same thing happening again, just in a different way?

"You are a good person," Noah said, his voice roughening, and he brushed her single tear away with the pad of his thumb before pulling her into a sudden, surprising, and much-needed hug.

Claire melted into that hug, her whole body softening and yielding to his. She needed another person's arms around her. Another person's total acceptance. She closed her eyes, feeling the hot press of the tears she'd held back against her lids. Put her arms around Noah and accepted his comfort and faith as if it were the only anchor in the drowning sea of her own emotions and guilt.

"Thank you," she finally whispered, easing back, too emotional to be embarrassed by what she'd said and shown. Maybe that would come later.

"Will you spend tomorrow with us?" Noah asked. "I don't know what we've got planned, but both Molly and I want to spend the day with you."

Claire gave him a wobbly smile. Her heart felt full of so many different emotions, but the one she could separate out from the rest was happiness. "I want that too," she said.

CHAPTER NINE

NOAH WOKE UP the next morning after a restless night and the first thought that flashed into his panic-stricken mind was that he hadn't bought a Christmas present for Molly.

He sat up in bed, driving a hand through his hair as he blinked sleep from his eyes. It was still pitch-dark out, not even five o'clock in the morning, but as a farmer he was up and dressed and out in the barn well before six. Now he swore quietly, regret lashing him. How could he have been so stupid, not to have a present for his daughter? It was Christmas *Eve*.

In years past he'd seen Molly the Saturday after Christmas, and he'd always picked her up something on the way into York. Not a possibility now and he should have realized before it was too late. Taking Molly to the shops to buy her own present on Christmas Eve was practically the definition of the hands-off, deadbeat dad.

With a groan aimed entirely at himself, Noah threw off the duvet and reached for his jeans. He made his way downstairs, fumbling in the dark, trying not to wake up

Molly. In the kitchen he fed Jake, who sprang to attention as soon as Noah put his foot on the bottom stair, and then put the kettle on to boil. He stood with one hip braced against the Aga, gazing unseeingly out the window at the unyielding darkness of a predawn winter, and thought of Claire.

He'd only known her for two days, and yet he'd shared more with her about Dani, about himself, than he had with anyone else. And he had a feeling she'd shared more with him about her own past, and that bastard Mark, than she had with anyone else.

Were they just two desperate and lonely people needing to unburden themselves, or did they share a real and surprising connection? Was he a fool for even asking the question?

Last night he'd come so very close to kissing her. He'd seen the awareness in her eyes, the way her lips had parted in expectation. They'd both wanted the kiss but he'd stepped back because…

Because, hell, this was complicated. He didn't want some fling, and he didn't know what else anything between him and Claire could be. They lived different lives on different continents. And, he reminded himself, they barely knew each other.

It just felt like they did. A lot.

The kettle started whistling and Noah made a mug of tea, brewing it dark and strong the way he liked and needed before heading out into the dark and cold. The temperature had raised enough to let the sheep out to graze, and he hoped he had time before Molly woke up to lead them to the high pasture where the snow had melted enough for them to roam in safety.

He left a note for her just in case, and then headed out into the freezing morning, Jake at his heels. It took an hour to move the sheep up, and it was still pitch-dark when he came back into the house at half past six. His body ached with fatigue; it had been a long, restless night spent thinking of Claire and imagining what would have happened if he had kissed her.

Molly hadn't stirred, so Noah set about making breakfast and counting down the hours until Claire would come back. They'd agreed last night they'd all spend the day together, but Noah knew his started a good deal earlier than Claire's. Yet the thought of waiting another four or five hours until she came over was torture.

You have it bad.

He made another cup of tea and fried some eggs, tidied the kitchen—a rather novel experience—and then paid some bills while he waited for Molly to wake up.

She came downstairs a little bit before eight, tousle-haired and sleepy-eyed, the sight of her both breaking and melting his heart.

"Hey, there." His voice sounded clogged and he cleared his throat. "Want some breakfast? I've got toast, cereal, eggs…"

"Toast." She slid onto a stool, watching him warily. "Is

Claire coming over today?"

"Yes." Noah popped two slices of bread in the toaster. "She's going to spend the day with us." He took a breath, let it out slowly. "But would it be so bad, Molly, if she didn't? If it was just the two of us?"

Molly didn't answer and Noah watched her pick at a split in the wooden worktop with one ragged fingernail. "I just like it when Claire is here," she said in a half-mumble.

"I do too," Noah answered, choosing his words with care. "She's a friend to both of us. But I love you, Molly. I love spending time with you, whether Claire is here or not."

She looked up then, her eyes bright and sparkling, Noah realized, with anger. "No, you don't." She spoke with such flat certainty that he felt a jolt of shock.

"Why do you think that?"

One bony shoulder lifted in a shrug. "Because you never see me."

"I see you every week—"

"For a couple of hours. You don't come to my plays or concerts. You don't take me on holidays. You don't *know* me. The only reason I'm spending Christmas with you is because Mum has a new boyfriend, and he doesn't like children." Her voice hitched and she wiped her nose with the sleeve of her pajamas. "It's not like you wanted me here," she finished and slipped off the stool.

Noah gaped at her, stunned and horrified by Molly's take on their relationship. In the silence, the sound of the toast popping up was joltingly loud.

Molly lifted her chin, her eyes sparkling now with tears. "I'm not hungry," she said, and left the room. Noah heard her bare feet slapping up the stairs, and then the distant slam of her door.

He stood there for a moment, Molly's words echoing through him. *You don't come to my plays or concerts. You don't take me on holidays. You don't know me.*

No, he didn't. He hadn't, he acknowledged for the first time, actually tried that hard.

It occurred to him then what a feeble excuse for a father he really was. He'd told Claire he'd been afraid to ask for a change in the custody arrangement, and while that was the truth, it wasn't quite the way he'd presented it to Claire.

He wasn't just afraid that Dani's parents would seek to reduce his time with Molly. He was afraid of messing up what he had with Molly, little as it was. Afraid of failing her, failing himself, failing as a dad. His track record at relationships wasn't stellar, after all, and a child was the greatest responsibility of all.

And you didn't even get her a present.

What an idiot he was. What a *jackass*.

No wonder Molly didn't have the time of day for him now. Wearily he took the toast out, spread it thickly with butter and jam, and took it upstairs as a peace offering. He didn't know what to say to Molly, but he knew he needed to say something.

He knocked once on the door, heard a muffled response, and opened it. Molly was sitting on her bed, leaning against the headboard, her knees tucked up with a notebook propped against her legs as she wrote or drew something madly.

"Just in case you're hungry," Noah said, and put the plate of toast on the bureau. Molly didn't answer. "Molly, I know I haven't been around as much as I should have been. Would have liked to have been." Molly made a sound like a snort and Noah sat on the edge of the bed. "The truth is…" How could he tell her the truth? She didn't know about his time in prison, or Dani's wild ways. She didn't know about the custody arrangement that kept him from seeing her more often. "The truth is," he started again, "your mum and I have had some difficulties, and part of that was when we both got to see you."

"And so you decided you didn't want to see me," she finished and Noah shook his head.

"It's not that simple."

"Seems it to me."

How, he wondered, could an eight-year-old have so many snappy comebacks?

"What if," he asked carefully, "I asked your Mum if I could see you more? Maybe you could spend the weekend here sometimes." It shamed him that he hadn't thought of this before now. Hadn't dared to.

Molly didn't answer.

"Do you like animals?" he asked. "You could help me in the barn if you wanted. But only if you wanted."

Molly still didn't speak and Noah forced himself to wait. "Would Claire be here?" she finally asked and his heart sank.

"I don't… no. Probably not. She lives in America, Molly."

Molly sniffed and looked away. The silence stretched on, seeming endless.

"Maybe," she finally said grudgingly, and Noah felt relief flood him, a cold, clear rush of feeling.

"Okay," he said. "I'll take maybe." He sat there for a moment more, but Molly didn't seem inclined to say anything else and so with an awkward pat of her knee he rose from the bed and went back downstairs.

As he came into the kitchen he heard a gentle tap on the back door, and another flood of relief rushed through him at the sight of Claire standing there.

"Good morning," she said with a shy duck of her head, and he couldn't keep from grinning back at her. Didn't even want to try.

"Good morning. I'm glad to see you." He had the strong impulse to hug her, the *need* to touch her, but despite coming so close to kissing her last night, he decided to keep his hands to himself. For now.

"How's Molly?" Claire asked as she came into the kitchen, unwinding a long, colorful scarf. Her cheeks were flushed with cold and she wore her long, dark hair in a high ponytail.

"She's okay. We had a talk."

"A talk?"

Noah raked a hand through his hair. "Just the start of one, really. She didn't think I wanted her here." Claire nodded, seeming unsurprised, and Noah asked, "Did you know that?"

"She told me something similar when I saw her over at Holly Cottage."

"Right."

She gave him a small, sympathetic smile. "Sorry."

"No, it's good. At least we're starting to have these conversations. I told her that maybe I could see about changing the custody arrangement, getting some more time with her."

"Do you think that could happen?"

"It should happen," Noah said, surprising himself with his fierceness. "Some of the things Molly has let slip make me think Dani's not doing as great a job as I hoped she was at motherhood. She's just throwing money at Molly, the same way her parents did to her."

"I know how that feels," Claire said quietly. "And as a kid, it's not good." Noah raised his eyebrows, wanting her to say more, and she continued hesitantly, "My parents were the same. We had a huge house, the best education, everything money could buy. My mother put on the most beautiful Christmases." The smile she gave him was twisted. "Designer tree, gourmet meal, the whole house decorated to the hilt."

"But?" Noah asked softly, because he knew there was one.

"But it felt so empty. I never felt like my parents cared about me, just about their image—our image, as this perfect family. They weren't interested in what I was doing or what I liked. They didn't spend any time with me. Every year the only present I ever got was an outfit to wear to the big, swanky New Year's Eve party we went to. And it was always an outfit I hated, some ridiculous frou-frou dress."

"Frou-frou dress," Noah said with an answering smile. "I haven't heard that one before. But I think I get the idea." He grimaced. "And speaking of presents, I haven't bought anything for Molly. That's how bad a dad I am."

"Remember that advice about not beating yourself up?" Claire reminded him.

"Yeah, I know. And you said it was hard to follow."

"Yes."

They gazed at one another for a moment, the silence spinning out, turning into something expectant and yet also wonderful. The silence of two people who understood each other. Noah's heart started to beat harder, and he wanted to say something of what he was feeling. But what?

Claire, I've only known you two days but I feel like we have something here.

What if she laughed him out of town? Or worse, what if her face crumpled in pity as she explained that there was no way anything could ever happen between them?

"Do you want some coffee?" he asked instead, his voice coming out kind of croaky, and Claire gave a nod.

"Sure."

"I checked and the Christmas Eve service is at four."

"I thought maybe we could bake cookies this morning. I can do it with Molly, I mean, if you need to do some stuff on the farm."

"I'm good. I could do a bit of biscuit baking."

"Biscuit," Claire said with a shake of her head. "I forgot. My godmother taught me a bunch of British words. I used to love hearing her speak."

"How is it that you have a British godmother?"

"She and my mom went to college together. They were best friends back then, but I think they've grown steadily apart since. Still, Ruth has been great about keeping in touch with me. Birthday and Christmas cards every year, and always an invitation to visit Ledstow."

"She's a nice lady."

"Yes, she is. I appreciate her letting me stay here."

"So do I."

They gazed at each other again, both smiling rather foolishly, and again Noah felt the need to say something.

Again he didn't.

CLAIRE HUMMED SOFTLY to herself as she retrieved the ingredients for cookies from Noah's cupboard. He had all the basics, thankfully, and she'd found a cookbook in a cupboard, dog-eared and lovingly worn.

As she paged through it to look for cookies recipes, she saw the notes written in a feminine hand in the margin, certain recipes circled or amended. She thought it was Noah's mother's handwriting, and she felt a little tug of loss at how different Noah's life must have been after his mother had died.

He came into the kitchen as she was flipping through the cookbook, and she looked up. "Was this your mother's?" she asked and he glanced down at it, frowning slightly.

"Yes, I suppose it was." He picked up the cookbook, leafing through it. "She liked to bake. She always had something for us, biscuits or flapjacks, after school."

"It must have been so hard when she died."

"Yeah." He closed the book, returning it to the counter. "It was."

"How did it happen?"

"Cancer. Less than six weeks from diagnosis to death. It was so fast I think our heads were all still spinning at the funeral." He shook his head slowly. "None of us had time to process it. I think that's why my dad shut down. Why David just wanted to leave."

And why Noah had found his escape through fun-loving Dani.

"I'm sorry."

"It was a long time ago."

"And how long have you been working on your own here at the farm?"

"I came back after I got out of prison, when I was twenty-one. I did some courses at college, but there wasn't the money or time for a degree. My dad died five years ago, from early-onset Alzheimer's. He'd been going downhill for a while before that, though."

"You've had a tough life, Noah."

He shrugged. "I'm luckier than some."

"That's not saying all that much."

"Don't feel too sorry for me," he said lightly, but she heard a warning in those words.

He didn't want her pity, and she could hardly blame him. She wouldn't want it either.

"I love living in Ledstow," he continued, "and Ayesgill Farm will always be my home."

And, Claire realized, there was a warning in those words, too. A reminder of how different their lives were, of how whatever was between them—and Claire wasn't remotely sure what that was—it wouldn't and couldn't go anywhere.

Not, at least, without one of them changing. A lot.

"I'll go get Molly," she murmured, and left Noah in the kitchen.

CHAPTER TEN

THEY MADE COOKIES in the morning, and ate the shortbread right out of the oven, burning their fingers. Then Claire found a CD of Christmas music, and they sang along to favorite carols and songs before heading outside to check on the sheep. Noah explained the basics of animals husbandry to Molly as they walked, gratified at how interested she seemed to be, thankful for Claire by his side.

It was, he decided, as he got ready for the Christmas Eve service at church, just about the best day he'd ever had.

It was already getting dark when they headed out in the Land Rover to the parish church in the middle of Ledstow. The narrow high street was strung with fairy lights, with a massive Christmas tree outside the village's lone pub, The Fair Maiden. Noah saw Claire smile at the decorations, and he wondered how Ledstow's few attractions would measure up to life in the big city.

For a day or a week, probably, village life would seem charming. But for longer? For a life?

And how on earth could he be thinking like that, so soon?

He parked the car on the high street across from the village post office shop; Claire glanced in its bow windows with a little smile before they all went through the lych-gate and then down the path that led to the church with its square Norman tower, the bells ringing out merrily, calling everyone to the service.

The church was nearly full as they entered, a massive Christmas tree at the front, and bunches of holly and evergreen tied to the end of each pew. Noah breathed in the scent of evergreen and dust and incense, a combination peculiar to the church and one that reminded him of his childhood. The last time he'd been in church, he realized, was for his mother's funeral.

As if sensing the nature of his thoughts, Claire glanced over and gave him a quick, reassuring smile. They all filed into a pew at the back and Noah glanced blindly down at his service sheet with its printed words to several well-known Christmas carols. *Silent night, holy night. All is calm, all is bright.*

The words fit, he thought, for his life right now. For once, things looked bright.

The service started and everyone stood to sing. Noah glanced around at the people in the church; he recognized a fair few of them as Ledstow lifers like he was. A lot of people, he realized, he hadn't connected with. Blokes he used to go to the pub with, for the occasional pint; friends of his mother's, who had baked them casseroles and pies when she had died. Somehow, over the lonely course of his life, he'd let them all slip away. Prison, he supposed, would do that to a person. Since getting out six and a half years ago, he hadn't wanted to show his face all that much. Everyone knew where he'd been, and he didn't know what they believed. Besides, he'd been dealing with his father's decline into Alzheimer's, and then just keeping the farm afloat.

Now, as he sung the words to the first hymn, *O Come All Ye Faithful*, he exchanged nods and smiles with a few of the people around him. Each one felt, in its own small way, like a blessing.

When he sat down again, he took Molly's hand. She glanced at him, surprised, but didn't pull away. And then, because he wanted to, he took Claire's hand, too. He even gave it a little squeeze.

She squeezed back and they sat there, the three of them in the pew, holding hands, while the music washed over him along with a deep, newfound peace.

CLAIRE HELD NOAH'S hand all through the service, and then took hold of Molly's afterwards, as they wandered back to the refreshment table where mini mince pies, shortbread, and punch had all been laid out. Noah had stayed back to chat with a man who looked about his age, and who had clapped him on the shoulder in greeting. Claire had the sense that this was big for Noah, that this wasn't just a casual friend he saw all the time, but some kind of homecoming. Smiling at Molly, they took a cookie each and went to look at the Sunday school display board.

The service had been beautiful. Claire couldn't remember when she'd last been to church, and certainly not a church like this, ancient and lovely, clearly a center of the community. A few people said hello and asked if she were visiting, and after getting into half a dozen friendly conversations, Noah rejoined them. He looked, Claire thought, rather adorably shell-shocked.

"Everything okay?" she asked.

"Yes. It's just been awhile since I've seen... well, anyone." He smiled ruefully. "I usually keep my head down, stay on the farm."

"Nice to get out?" Claire surmised, her eyebrows raised, and Noah nodded.

"When we get home," Molly asked, tugging on both their hands, "can we hang our stockings?"

Noah and Claire exchanged glances. Neither of them had discussed what would happen after today, if Claire would spend Christmas with them. And while just yesterday she had been worried about whether she was insinuating herself into Noah and Molly's lives, wondering if she were being stupid or desperate or both, now the answer seemed easy. Obvious.

"I suppose we can," she told Molly. "If we have stockings?"

"There might be some up in the storage loft," Noah answered. "We had them when I was a kid."

"Then the answer is yes," Claire said, glancing at Noah just to make sure, and he nodded. When they'd all got in the old Land Rover, Claire asked him, "Are there any special traditions your family had for Christmas Eve? Special meals or...?"

"We always had shepherd's pie on Christmas Eve," Noah said with a little laugh. "I'd forgotten that. Kind of an in-joke."

"Shepherds eating shepherd's pie," Claire surmised with a smile. "While they watched their flocks by night."

"All seated on the ground," Noah answered solemnly, and Claire let out a laugh.

"I don't even know what Christmas carol that is."

"I think it's actually called 'While Shepherds Watched Their Flocks by Night.'"

"That makes sense."

Both laughed again, grinning at each other like goons, while Molly piped up, "I have no idea what you're talking about."

Back at the farm, Noah went to find the stockings while Claire looked in his mother's cookbook for the recipe for shepherd's pie. It looked like a simple dish of ground beef or lamb mixed with gravy and topped with mashed potatoes. Molly helped her to make it, peeling potatoes and chopping an onion. They worked in happy, quiet companionship, and a few minutes later Noah came into the kitchen, bearing a box.

"I found the stockings."

"Let's see," Molly cried, and Claire caught the half-peeled potato that threatened to roll off the counter. Noah withdrew several Christmas stockings from the box; Claire could see how lovingly they'd been made, hand-knit with pictures stitched on each—lambs for the boys, a ram for the father and a ewe for his mother.

"Oh, they're so sweet," she exclaimed and Molly took one of the stockings decorated with a lamb. "Can I have this one?"

"Of course," Noah said, and briefly rested his hand on top of Molly's head.

They hung the stockings in front of the fireplace in the sitting room while they waited for the shepherd's pie to cook. Claire sat on the sofa with Noah while Molly carefully hung hers, arranging it this way and that. Noah had draped his arm along the back of the sofa, and his fingers were just barely brushing Claire's shoulder. She was acutely aware of that tiny touch, longed to lean into it, into him, and rest her head against his shoulder. She resisted, but only just.

They ate at the big pine table in the kitchen, and Noah got out some candles from the box of Christmas decorations and put them in the middle, along with some holly and evergreen for a centerpiece.

As Claire sat down, the candlelight flickering over Noah

and Molly's faces, she marveled at how she'd got to this point. She wanted to tell Noah this was the best Christmas she'd ever had, but she was afraid it might sound too silly, too eager.

But maybe it was time to stop feeling afraid.

They ate dinner and Claire washed up while Noah took Molly out to the barn. She stood in the middle of the tidy kitchen, one hand resting on the railing of the Aga, and thought, *I could like this. I could live like this.*

New York City and her job at Stirling, felt far away, as distant as the moon, and just as cold and barren. Would she miss her friends if she left New York? Yes, of course she would.

Would you miss Noah more? And Molly?

"You are being crazy," she said aloud.

There could be no denying that this time with Noah and Molly was special, even magical. But it was Christmas and they'd both been alone, and it didn't necessarily mean that anything they were feeling was actually real. That it could last.

The back door opened and Noah and Molly came in, stamping the snow from their boots.

Claire turned to them with a smile, and tried her best to banish her crazy thoughts.

A little while later Noah got Molly settled in bed and Claire sat curled up on the sofa in front of the fire in the sitting room. She'd thought about leaving when Noah and

Molly had gone upstairs, but she'd been reluctant to go back to Holly Cottage and spend the evening alone and… well. Pretty much that.

Noah came downstairs, smiling as he caught sight of her sitting there before clapping a hand to his forehead, his expression turning to one of almost comical dismay.

"I still don't have a present for Molly!"

"Oh, no." Claire frowned. They'd been so busy doing Christmassy things, they'd forgotten about presents. Not, she acknowledged, that presents were that important, but… Molly needed something under the tree.

Noah came and sank onto the sofa next to her. "I thought about a present this morning, but I didn't do anything about it. I didn't want to just take her out to the shops and have her pick something. That seemed so soulless."

"There must be something," Claire said. "It doesn't have to cost a lot of money. Trust me, I know that. It's the thought that counts, as trite as that can sound."

"And I haven't put any thought into it," Noah said. His face set into resigned lines. "The truth is, until this week, I've been a pretty nothing dad."

"You didn't have a lot of opportunity—"

"Even so. I could have pressed for more time with Molly. I could have made our Saturdays more special somehow. I just kept it the way it was because…" He trailed off, shaking his head.

Claire prompted softly, "Because?"

"Because I was so overwhelmed with everything else," Noah said on a sigh. "With caring for my dad and taking care of the farm. And because I was scared of messing things up. Messing her up."

"That's understandable."

"Still doesn't make it right."

"No."

They were silent for a moment, their legs brushing as they sat on the sofa, the only sound the crackle of the fire as the logs settled in the grate.

Finally Noah turned to her, smiling tiredly. "So what am I going to do? What can I give her?"

"Do you know what she's interested in?"

He shrugged, helpless. "Dolls? Toys? She looked like she was drawing earlier, when I went up to her bedroom."

"She was drawing when I saw her over by Holly Cottage yesterday morning," Claire said. "Maybe something to do with that?"

"The shops are closed—"

"She might like something that was yours when you were little," Claire suggested. "A piece of her history."

"Something old and tatty, then."

"It really won't matter to her, Noah. Trust me."

"I suppose I need another trip to the storage loft." He rose from the sofa and reluctantly Claire uncurled her legs and started to stand up.

"I suppose I should go—"

"No, not yet," Noah said quickly. "Not until I have this present figured out."

She sat back down, curling up again, so easily convinced. "Okay."

Noah went upstairs and Claire leaned back against the sofa, enjoying the flickering flames of the fire, the sense of comfort and peace that pervaded the house. After a few minutes she went to make coffee, and she'd just come back into the living room with two steaming mugs when Noah came down the stairs.

"I found my old art set," he said with a rueful grin. He held out the tin case, tarnished and dented. "Like I said, old and tatty."

"And perfect." Claire handed him a mug of coffee. "And I had an idea too. What about giving her a new notebook? I saw some in one of the drawers of the dresser in the kitchen—"

"You think that's enough?" Noah asked a little dubiously.

"What if you decorated it? With things that mattered to you?"

Noah looked even more dubious. "Decorated it…"

"It's called decoupage," Claire told him with a laugh. "I could help you. We could use photos, colored paper, some of the silver glitter that you were so fond of with the pinecones."

"As long as you'll help," Noah answered.

They set up at the kitchen table, collecting as many craft items as Noah could find around the house, glue and tape, and some old photos he didn't mind cutting up. Claire had just spread it all out when Noah came to the table, a bottle of whiskey in his hand.

"I think we'll need this too," he told her solemnly. "Fancy a splash in your coffee?"

"Yes, please," Claire said and Noah poured a generous amount in both mugs.

They spent a companionable hour arranging photos and pictures on the cover of the notebook while drinking whisky-laced coffee and chatting about nothing too important. By ten o'clock the notebook was finished; there were photos of Noah as a boy and of Ayesgill Farm; pictures cut out from magazines of lambs and sheep; a few random sequins he'd found in the back of a drawer, and of course the silver glitter. Covered with clear contact paper, it looked surprisingly polished.

"This actually looks kind of amazing," Noah said as they gazed at the finished notebook. "Thanks to you."

"You had something to do with it," Claire answered.

She turned to him just as Noah turned to her, so their noses nearly bumped. Claire felt as if the whole room had just shivered, as if the very air around them had suddenly tautened. She could hear the sudden pop and crack of the fire in the other room as it burned down to embers, just as something flared vitally to life between them, right here.

Claire's lips parted and her heart started thumping hard. Everything in her quivered with awareness and expectation. Noah's gaze dropped to her mouth, and her heart thumped harder, and then...

Then he kissed her.

The feel of his lips on hers was a shock, and yet also so wonderfully right. Her hands bunched in his shirt as she yielded to his kiss, her whole body thrumming with sensation and desire. Noah slid his hands up to cradle her face as he deepened the kiss.

Distantly Claire heard the scrape of a chair's legs on the floor, the clatter of some of the craft supplies falling from the table. None of it mattered.

All she could feel, all she could want, was Noah's kiss. His mouth on hers. His hands on her body.

She nearly groaned aloud when he slid his hand to cup her breast, his fingers warm and seeking through her cashmere top.

Then suddenly he stopped, withdrawing his hand, easing back to look at her seriously. "Claire..." he said, and though he'd only said her name, she knew what he was asking. Knew too what she wanted.

"Yes," she said and with a smile of relief Noah laced his fingers through hers and led her upstairs.

CHAPTER ELEVEN

C LAIRE FOLLOWED NOAH down the hallway and into his bedroom; the moonlight spilled from the window, illuminating a large, masculine bed with a rumpled navy duvet and a headboard that looked as if it had been crafted from a barn beam.

He turned, tugging her to him by the hand, and kissed her again. Claire kissed him back, everything in her wanting and needing this connection. The scrape of his stubbled chin against her cheek. The feel of his hands sliding down her body, underneath her top. The life-giving touch of his mouth on hers.

She slipped her hands under his shirt, savoring the feel of his taut, muscled chest, the crisp hair tickling her fingers.

"I changed the sheets," Noah murmured with a hoarse little laugh, "in case you're wondering."

Claire raised her eyebrows as she slid her hands down to the waistband of his jeans and popped the button. "So you were hoping to get lucky?"

"Maybe on a subconscious level," Noah admitted with a grin. "Actually, maybe not so subconscious."

She laughed, and he did too, and then urgency took over and their clothes started flying as they scrambled to get naked.

Noah led her to the bed, pulled her down with him onto the rumpled duvet, and Claire went eagerly, joyfully. She curved her body around his, arched up to meet his caress, and felt like she'd never need or want anything ever again.

SHE WOKE TO pitch darkness, but Noah was already up, tiptoeing across the room as he searched for his clothes. Claire glanced at the clock and saw it was just a little past five in the morning. She half-rose from the bed, clutching the duvet to her, and Noah glanced over.

"Sheep," he said succinctly, and she sank back against the pillows.

"Right."

Neither of them said anything more, just gazed at each other through the darkness. Claire couldn't tell if it was awkward or not. Was she the only one feeling unsure, a little embarrassed?

"Molly…" Noah finally began, and unwelcome realization flooded through her. Of course. Noah wouldn't want Molly to wake up and see Claire in his bed.

"Right," she said again, and sat up, still clutching the duvet. Somehow being naked now felt more revealing than it had last night. Noah must have sensed that for he yanked on his clothes quickly.

"I'll be back around six," he said and Claire just nodded. "There's a spare bedroom down the hall, if you want to catch some more sleep," he added, and she could definitely tell now that it was awkward. Very awkward. She nodded again, and Noah left.

Claire pulled back the duvet and scrambled for her clothes. As early as it was, she didn't think she'd be able to sleep anymore now, and so she got dressed, brushed her teeth with her finger and a little toothpaste, and headed downstairs.

The kitchen was dark and quiet; Noah had thankfully already gone out. Claire filled the kettle and plonked it on the Aga, trying to sort through the tangle of feelings that had lodged in her chest in a burning lump. None of them, at this moment, felt good.

Last night had, she acknowledged, been wonderful. Tender and passionate and just...

She closed her eyes, reliving those moments when Noah had joined his body with hers, when she'd felt so complete and whole and loved.

This morning seemed to make a mockery of it all.

She told herself not to be stupid, that Noah had been being sensible when he warned her about Molly. *Of course* she couldn't wake up in his bed. She knew that. She understood it, agreed with it. Yet it still made everything feel sordid and... wrong.

The kettle started whistling and Claire yanked it off the stove. She was telling herself not to panic, that it hadn't been sordid, but she could barely hear that calm voice of reason over the million alarm bells clanging through her head. The alarm bells that were insisting what had happened between them hadn't been meaningful or real, that everything was flimsy and fake. Nothing more than a holiday fling.

And maybe she'd have been okay with that, if she hadn't started to care so much. If she weren't halfway to falling in love with Noah, or even farther along that dangerous road.

She drew a ragged breath, swallowed past the lump of emotion that had risen in her throat. She made herself a cup of tea and drank it while staring sightlessly out the window; it was still pitch-black.

Memories were starting to creep into her mind like malevolent ghosts. Memories of Mark, of creeping from his apartment, shamed and heartsick, not wanting to wake Emma. Of turning around and seeing sixteen-year-old Emma standing in the doorway of her bedroom in her pajamas, her face pale and shocked.

Emma had never said anything to Claire about finding her teacher in her apartment at one o'clock in the morning, and Claire had never spoken of it either. But she'd lived in the shadow of that moment since it had happened five weeks ago. Lived and grieved.

This is different, her heart insisted. Noah wasn't married, for a start. And what they'd shared, short as the time had been, had been special for both.

You thought what you had with Mark was special.

Claire closed her eyes, the cup of tea forgotten in her hand. Could she trust her instincts, her heart, at all? Falling for Mark, convincing herself, even for a short time, that it didn't matter that he was married, that his wife didn't care about him or Emma, had shown her how easily she was willing to deceive herself.

She heard the creak of the back door and Claire opened her eyes. Noah had come into the kitchen, his cheeks ruddy from cold, his hair ruffled. He smiled when he saw her.

"I thought you'd still be in bed."

The spare room bed. "I couldn't sleep."

He took a step towards her, his face softening. "Happy Christmas."

Christmas. It was Christmas morning. Somehow she'd forgotten. And somehow it made her feel worse. "I should go." Surprised flashed across Noah's features. "I need to take a shower, change my clothes." She gestured to her jeans and sweater. "I'm wearing the same thing as yesterday. Molly might notice."

Claire saw the moment realization and acceptance dawned on Noah's face, and even though she'd expected it, it still crushed her. Suddenly it hurt to breathe.

"Okay," he said. "But we'll see you later?"

"Yes," she said, but it felt like a lie. "Yes, of course you will."

NOAH WATCHED CLAIRE yank on her coat and boots before hurrying outside. Belatedly he realized he hadn't kissed her goodbye, hadn't offered to run her back in his Land Rover. He hadn't time to process... anything. And now she was gone.

What the hell had just happened?

Something had, of that Noah was sure. In between the magic of last night and the mess of this morning, something had changed, and he wasn't sure what.

He didn't like it. He wanted to get out of the awful awkwardness, and get back the tenderness and passion he'd shared with Claire last night. Maybe the morning after was bound to be awkward. Maybe Claire regretted...

But, no. He wouldn't let himself think like that. He'd stay positive. Hopeful. It had been a long time since he'd had anything to hope for.

He heard the clatter of Molly coming down the stairs, and turned to greet her, forcing a smile onto his face.

"Happy Christmas, Moll."

His little girl hurled herself into his arms, surprising Noah and making his heart sing even as the worries and doubts about Claire whispered in his mind. "Happy Christmas, Dad," she said, and before Noah could say anything else, she slid out of his arms and looked around the empty kitchen. "Where's Claire?"

"She's at her place, Molly."

"But..." Molly frowned, the happiness in her eyes winking out like a candle. "I thought she was spending Christmas with us."

"She is," Noah assured his daughter, although suddenly he didn't feel so sure. "But it's still early."

Molly nodded slowly, and Noah hated how her thin little shoulders slumped in defeat. Hated how his insides jolted with fear and disappointment and heartache. Hell, he didn't want to wait for Claire to come back to him. She'd been spooked by what had happened, the reality of the morning after, just as he had been. He got that. But he also got that Christmas wasn't Christmas without Claire.

"I've got an idea," he told Molly, and she looked up warily. "How about we go over to Holly Cottage and wish Claire a Happy Christmas?" Molly's face brightened and Noah continued, "And then we'll bring back her here."

CLAIRE TRUDGED THROUGH the heavy, melting snow, blinking back tears and hating how hurt she felt. How heartbroken. It was surely too much emotion for a man she'd met a handful of days ago.

That's just an excuse. You're falling in love with Noah, and he doesn't feel the same way about you. How could he?

She wrenched open the door to Holly Cottage, kicking off her boots and fighting the urge to scream into the silence.

None of it was real. None of it was meant to last.

The voices in her head were insistent, mocking, awful.

Claire put her hands to her ears as if she could stop them, but of course she couldn't. And so she did the only thing she could do, the one thing she needed to do.

She cried.

The sobs came from a place deep inside her, huge wrenching gulps that tore at her soul. She was, she knew, crying for so many things—her lonely childhood, her wretched almost-affair with Mark, her pseudo-relationship with Noah. All of it.

She didn't know how long she cried only that she'd collapsed into an armchair, the sobs having subsided to sniffles, when she heard a knock on the door.

With a cold ripple of shock she saw the outlines of two figures through the frosted glass—Noah and Molly.

Hurriedly Claire wiped at her cheeks, but a quick glance in the mirror told her that she wouldn't be fooling anybody. Her eyes were puffy and red, her face swollen. Taking a deep breath, she opened the door.

Noah jerked back when he saw her, clearly surprised by how awful she looked, but Molly barely noticed, just wrapped her arms around Claire's middle.

"Happy Christmas, Claire!" she sang out, and Claire met Noah's gaze over Molly's head. Something silent passed between them; Claire suspected Noah knew why she was crying, and she didn't know how she felt about that.

"We came to bring you back home," Molly explained, and at that simple, heartfelt statement, Claire nearly started crying again.

She went upstairs to change, and a few minutes later walked back across the snowy fields to Ayesgill Farm. Stepping inside the cozy kitchen, the whole house smelling of pine and evergreen, really did feel like coming home.

As soon as they'd got inside, Molly rushed to open her stocking, which Claire and Noah had filled with an assortment of candy and small toys they'd found around the house. Nothing particularly showy or special, but Molly seemed delighted with it all.

Noah looked worried at the single wrapped present under the tree, but Molly didn't seem to care that she only had one. And the look on her face when she saw the notebook and Noah explained about her drawing...

It was almost another time for tears.

After Molly had gone upstairs to put away her notebook and stocking stuff, Claire went into the kitchen to figure out Christmas dinner. Noah had bought a turkey, and she thought she could manage a few side dishes. She wasn't sure what they'd do about dessert...

"Claire."

Claire stilled, her back to Noah, everything in her tensing in expectation and fear. Was he going to thank her, then let her down gently? It would be so, so awful...

"Please," she managed. "Don't say anything."

Noah was silent for a moment and, steeling herself, Claire turned around. She couldn't tell a thing from his face.

"What do you think I'm going to say?" he finally asked and she shrugged jerkily.

"Something along the lines of 'thanks for the memories', I guess."

"I want more for my life than memories," Noah answered, and Claire just blinked at him. "I know things have happened fast between us," he continued steadily. "Really fast. It's been crazy and intense and wonderful, and while I know this feels like a break from real life, what I've felt for you, what you've made me feel…" He paused and Claire just watched him, her heart beating so hard it hurt. "It makes me want to try real life with you. However we can do that."

"How…" Claire whispered, although she didn't even know what she was asking, only that she was so, so glad about what Noah had said.

"I don't know how," Noah admitted with a crooked smile. "However we can. You flying here. Me flying to New York City. I've always wanted to go to America. I know," he continued before she could so much as frame a word, "It's not ideal. And that at some point, if we—if things become serious, we'll have to make some choices. All I'm asking is for a chance to get to that point. To see what this thing between us can become, can grow into, if we let it."

"I want that," Claire whispered. "So much. But I know things are complicated, with Molly…"

"Molly loves you," Noah answered. "That's pretty obvious. And yes, things are complicated. But not too complicated, I hope."

"Not too complicated," Claire whispered.

Noah's grin broke through, making Claire grin back at him. "Then come here, woman, and let me kiss you."

And she did, relishing how he enveloped her in his arms, how his lips felt so right on hers.

Distantly Claire heard the patter of footsteps, and then an audible gasp.

"*Oh*!" Molly exclaimed, and then she giggled. "This is the best Christmas *ever!*"

EPILOGUE

One year later...

CLAIRE CRANED HER head to look out of the tiny airplane window, but all she could see was endless darkness. They were only three hours out of New York, but already she was tapping her foot, everything in her fizzing with anticipation at being back in Ledstow again.

It was hard to believe in some ways that she'd been on a plane just like this one a year ago, heartsick and lonely, wanting only solitude. And returned to New York a week later, her life utterly changed. She'd picked up the same airline magazine she'd flipped through on the way out, read, with a little smile on her face, all the twenty-five tips to a perfect Christmas *BrambleCottage.com* had advised. The website had saved the best for last: *Spend Christmas with the ones you love.* Well, Claire had certainly done that. Amazingly.

The year since then had been life-changing and wonderful, yet not without its share of difficulties.

She and Noah had begun a transatlantic relationship, with one of them flying over to the other every six weeks.

Claire had ended up going to Ledstow more than Noah had come to New York, because of the responsibilities at the farm, but also because Claire simply preferred Ledstow to city life. And when the time had come to make a decision, it had been easy for each of them. Claire would move to Ledstow, and she'd enrolled in a course at York University to get her teaching qualification in England. She and Noah would marry in the church where he'd first held her hand, the Saturday after Christmas.

Claire sat back in her seat, a smile curving her mouth as she thought of all that had changed. Noah had asked for more time with Molly, and in May he'd been granted school holidays and every other weekend. His relationship with Molly had had its fair share of setbacks, but it was stronger now than it ever had been.

Claire had made peace with her own past, apologizing to Emma for her almost-affair with her father, and finally forgiving herself.

And now the future loomed in front of her, bright and shining. Her family was even coming to England for the wedding; her mother had decided on a 'Dickens Christmas', whatever that meant. Claire had made her peace with them too, in the quiet of her own heart.

Three hours later the plane landed in Manchester, and Claire speed-walked towards Immigration, desperate to get out of the airport and see Noah and Molly. She'd told him not to bother coming to Manchester to get her; she could rent a car, and he had too many responsibilities with the farm. Just a few more hours, she thought. *A few more hours until I see him.*

Immigration took longer than usual, but she brandished her new permission-to-remain visa, collected her bags and breezed through Customs. Now just to pick up the rental car and drive to Ledstow.

Claire stopped short at the sight of Noah and Molly standing by the Customs exit with the private car drivers brandishing their signs with various surnames. Noah and Molly had a sign too—*Welcome Home*.

Grinning from ear to ear, her heart full to overflowing, Claire walked towards her family.

THE END

THE WILLOUGHBY CLOSE SERIES

Discover the lives and loves of the residents of Willoughby Close

The four occupants of Willoughby Close are utterly different and about to become best friends, each in search of her own happy ending as they navigate the treacherous waters of modern womanhood in the quirky yet beautiful village of Shipstow, nestled in the English Cotswolds...

Book 1: A Cotswold Christmas

Book 2: Meet Me at Willoughby Close

Book 3: Find me at Willoughby Close

Book 4: Kiss Me at Willoughby Close

Book 5: Marry Me at Willoughby Close

ABOUT THE AUTHOR

After spending three years as a diehard New Yorker, **Katharine Swartz** now lives in the Lake District in England with her husband, their five children, and a Golden Retriever. She enjoys such novel things as long country walks and chatting with people in the street, and her children love the freedom of village life—although she often has to ring four or five people to figure out where they've gone off to.

She writes women's fiction as well as contemporary romance under the name Kate Hewitt, and whatever the genre she enjoys delivering a compelling and intensely emotional story.

You can find out more about Katharine on her website at www.kate-hewitt.com.

Thank you for reading

A Yorkshire Christmas

If you enjoyed this book, you can find more from all our great authors at TulePublishing.com, or from your favorite online retailer.

TULE
PUBLISHING

Printed in Great Britain
by Amazon